CONCLUSION

A NOVEL

PETER ROBERTSON

GIBSON HOUSE PRESS

CHICAGO

ALSO BY PETER ROBERTSON

Permafrost

Mission

Colorblind

FOR MY FAMILY

RUBY

Death was less than an hour away.

At the halfway mark on the mansion walk, with the sun high and unforgiving overhead and the promise of shade on the path ahead an unconvincing notion, Colin and Ruby Tugdale allowed themselves a break.

With fewer than four weeks of pristine health remaining, Ruby Tugdale joined the line outside the solitary port-a-potty, while her husband, Colin, sat and waited for her, perched on a low stone wall, his back stoic and straight, his chosen angle a snub to the expanse of glass-like ocean.

Colin enjoyed walking, but today both of his feet hurt. Today his heart was all but crushed, and his pains, both physical and emotional, were not lessened by the queue for the potty, which offered a cruel study in motionlessness.

As he continued to sit with his back to the ocean, Colin's eyes fell with a sense of certainty on a bike lock impotently attached to the chain-link fence that surrounded a veritable palace: three extravagant stories of green marble fortress offered up to the gilded gods of all things gaudy and gauche.

The lock on the fence provided Colin a welcome distraction, both from the pain in his feet and from the purpose of their walk. According to the designs and machinations of the prevailing government, Colin Tugdale was less than a month away from becoming a weld widower. But in this belief, the authorities were mistaken, because Colin's year of widower-hood would commence much sooner. Within the next hour, if the Tugdales had planned Ruby's pre-conclusion correctly.

Colin got to his feet and walked over to the fence. He lifted the lock. He looked at it. The black paint was chipped and the lock cheaply manufactured, yet the mechanism was rust free. He yanked twice at it, but it held fast. He had known that it would be locked, as he had known it would resist him. As he also knew that when he aligned the four numbers, it would spring open for him.

Because all he had to do was to know the combination of numbers. And strangely, he did. The combination was two-three-eight-one. Colin was as certain of this as he had been certain of anything in his life. Seconds later, the lock lay open in his hand.

His soon-to-be forever-dead Ruby had silently returned to his side. He placed the lock in his trouser pocket. She watched him but said nothing.

A moment later she favored him with what would be one of her final fathomless looks. It grasped at all that remained of his heart.

"We should probably keep going," she said quietly.

He heard her and nodded once. "How are you feeling?"

"I feel fine. But then that was the whole point of every-thing. Wasn't it?"

The Tugdales had visited this tourist town once before. A week of beach walks and seafood and sightseeing and a two-day festival of teeming rain and music during which, by their delighted calculations, their only son, Tony, had been conceived. As they sat warm and steaming in their soaked clothes, the festival parking lot an ocean of mud, the occluded windows of their rented car contributed to the overall sense of freedom that bad wine and the cheap weed had set off.

When Ruby Tugdale was fifty-four, her son was twenty-five. He had been to college, been in love exactly twice, and had been diagnosed with type 1 diabetes at the age of nine. There was no known cure, but, armed with insulin inhalers and cutting-edge digital technology that read his insulin levels on skin contact, Tony faced the pleasurable probability of decent health and a more-than-respectable lifespan, but with his flawed genetic makeup, he would be afforded no possibility of a Geneweld.

For Ruby and Colin this was worrisome, but they had little choice but to accept it. What was a harder pill to swallow for his parents was their son's career prospects—or lack thereof. Tony returned to the Tugdale roost post-college and took up residence in the basement. He played computer games and he slept and he ate, seemingly in that order of importance.

The Tugdales were comfortable but by no means wealthy people. So, they conspired, and they calculated. They reasoned that two Weld Wads would buttress Tony's uncertain future. Ruby taught ice skating and Colin ran the IT department for a small school district. They lived carefully within their means and vacationed together only occasionally, even though Colin enjoyed close to two months of summer vacation time, during which he walked briskly across low mountain ranges alone and taught a novice computer science class to frail non-welds at a local community center. Welds were never frail. They were also largely more tech knowledgeable, for reasons Colin Tugdale could never fully understand.

Within the span of two years, the Tugdales were scanned, welded, and given their settlements, which they placed in Tony's mostly empty bank account. Two months after Colin was welded, the beta version of Trench Warfare, a first-person shooter game, hit the gaming market. In an instant, the shy creator, one Anthony Tugdale, was the toast of the gaming world and a young man who would never encounter a money worry, even if he managed to live forever.

Playing TW Basic online cost nothing. Upgrading the nerve gases, the armored tanks, the machine guns, the waterproof trench wear, and the other World War One–appropriate game add-ons required either superlative gaming skills or an online account with readily available funds.

Tony would never need his parents' money. He tried to give it back numerous times. He was turned down at first, but after his umpteenth hack into their bank account, Colin and Ruby gave up and left this injection of cash to languish undisturbed.

Ruby told Tony that she would have chosen the weld even without the worry of his future. She was happy to live to seventy-five in perfect health. She told Colin they would live as they had always lived, and Colin and Tony saw no reason to argue with Ruby on these or any other points.

Colin Tugdale was glad his son was rich. He had helped Tony with some of the technology as the game had developed. He cherished their time spent together, even if it was mostly spent in the basement. It had never occurred to Colin that their tinkering would produce a gaming sensation, and he also couldn't help being surprised that so many adolescent gamers enjoyed the digital recreation of what was arguably the most static and tedious of military encounters.

Colin wasn't afraid of death or pain or illness. When he was young, he had assumed that all three would make an unwelcome appearance at some point; now there would only be one.

He had always known that Ruby would go first. Now he wished he could change the order.

You need to enjoy your time alone, she had told him more than once.

The world's first genetic welding had taken place in the research laboratory of a small English university with questionable academic credentials and a financial nest thatched with cash from a local landowning family.

First there was the genome scanning of monkeys, followed by genetic welding, in which strands of primate DNA were welded in place. Some of the unsuspecting patients had been scanned and pronounced healthy, while others, for control purposes, had been scanned and pronounced less than healthy.

This bold if reckless act of biological imagining occurred with little fanfare. Similarly, the lengthy second act took place in anonymity. The university researchers watched and waited while twenty years passed. Some of the welded trial monkeys lived, and some died, the dying occasioned by a number of messily unscientific reasons, over a decidedly non-scientific spectrum of time.

Of greater interest was that all the primates that had been scanned and certified healthy before their weld subsequently lived a uniform twenty years in perfect health. Then they all died, in a gentle, painless, and unremarkable manner. They simply ceased to live, and all within the first few weeks of what would have been their twenty-first year post-weld. In addition to their uniformly good health, and the rigid cluster of their deaths, was the fact that all the certified-healthy monkeys had failed to age a single day in the passing of two decades.

There were outliers and anomalies. Two certified monkeys consumed spoiled vegetables and died well before their All Clear Twenty had passed. One certified female monkey died from pregnancy complications. Several monkeys who had failed the scan outlived their certified counterparts by a number of years. But they were the lucky ones. And they still aged. And they still got very sick in the end.

When the research team called for human volunteers for the scan/weld combo, there was a stampede. Some were robust specimens. Others proved less hardy. As with their simian ancestors, the volunteers who passed the scan and subsequently received the weld lived for twenty years, once again pain free, disease free, and relieved of the bothersome business of physical or mental aging.

Like their evolutionary forebears, the healthy volunteers were by no means assured immortality with their welds. They still crashed their cars and drank to liver-destroying excess and shot each other over matters of love and money. But if they managed to avoid these often-lethal distractions, they passed away at a juncture easy to calculate, in a manner unexplained and yet peaceful in its precise inevitability.

The unhealthy volunteers, cursed as they were with any one of myriad preexisting conditions, lived and died as a result of their preexisting conditions. Some within the twenty years. Some well beyond. Some died a blessedly good death. Some expired in a less-blessed manner. But all lived a life accompanied by the usual aches and pains and accumulated collections of sags and bulges and lines and wrinkles.

As with the primates, what was most interesting about the lifespans of the healthy volunteers was their failure to age at all during two pain-free and idyllic decades following their welds.

All this science made headlines. In the years when the first patients were scanned and approved, pharmaceutical company fortunes were giddily anticipated, insurance actuaries calculated and conferred, and eager hospitals were requisitioned, as the governments of the world wrestled with the costs and the benefits and, less enthusiastically, with the moral and cultural implications.

There was vigorous debate over when to apply the Geneweld. A human specimen in the full vigor of their twenties could remain in good health for twenty more years. But then they would die relatively young. Whereas a man or woman in his or her dotage could now painlessly reach the century mark and still possess the spryness of a whippersnapper of eighty.

While more than a handful of zealots railed against the fundamental ungodliness of the concept, it was strenuously argued that securing a lifespan just in excess of three score and ten was well in line with Old Testament guidelines.

The question of when to scan and weld thus became a contentious issue, until the powerful governments of the world stepped in and resolved the matter. At fifty-five years of age, all who chose to be were scanned, and few passed on the free test. The scan took less than thirty minutes to produce a definitive answer, and the weld usually took place overnight very soon thereafter.

In the case of wealthier countries, the weld was accompanied by a lump-sum payment calculated on a complex matrix of needs and earning potential and the savings incurred by not paying for medicine and not keeping someone marginally alive for the near-century that the wonders of modern science could now theoretically achieve.

To obtain prior knowledge of the time of your death was a curious life- and death-altering experience. Many who were close to concluding opted to select their own time, deciding on a moment a little ahead of time. Their suicides—pre-conclusions—were either simple or elaborately staged events taking place at locations rife with special meaning. Others chose to wait to the very last to fall into that mysterious final sleep. For those who waited, there were minor aberrations. Their twenty years would mysteriously end, seldom more than a day or two beyond, but never ever less than the allotted two decades.

Colin and Ruby started to walk the second half of the shore path, across the uneven, rectangular rocks blanched chalk white by the sea salt, toward a yellow crumbling brick wall, through the corrugated metal tunnel with the damp, mossy floor naturally inlaid with smooth pebbles, and out past the last garish bastions perched on the steep cliffside.

When they emerged from the tunnel, the path narrowed and ascended steeply. Colin grasped the lock tightly in his pocket as he began to climb.

The lock numbers were two-three-eight-one. Two-three-eight-one. Two-three-eight-one. They took on the aspect of a mantra.

"We're getting close now." Her words had several meanings.

"I could always . . ."

She shook her head. "No, you couldn't. We already talked about it. And we already agreed."

"It would be easy enough."

She was adamant. "We planned it this way."

You planned it this way, was what he thought. "I know we did."

They continued to climb.

She smiled at him. "You might even like your time alone."

"And I might not."

"So, what will you do?"

"Walk, I suppose," he shrugged. "I do like to walk."

"You should read. You should do something different. You don't ever read."

Colin pretended to consider this. "Perhaps I will read then."

"And you will see Tony often."

"And I will see Tony often."

Ruby changed the subject. "Afterward, you will take me to the garden. And to the beach."

The path came to an end. There was a warning sign, but it was unnecessary. The path simply wasn't. There was the comfort of a bench on one side and on the other nothing but the sky falling into the rocks underneath and the salt water lapping gently further away.

Ruby had carried the backpack the whole way. She had insisted on that. They sat down on the bench. She opened the wine with a cheap corkscrew. Dark red wine from some-where in the middle of France. It was the oldest and most expensive vintage they had ever purchased. She handed Colin both glasses and she poured. Her hand began to shake, and he turned away. The first of her last tears glistened on her cheek.

When she finished pouring, they let their glasses clash clumsily. And then they drank.

"It's too warm. It should taste better than this."

"It's fine," he said too hastily.

She shook her head slowly. "It's hopeless. I can't drink any more. I'm so scared."

"I can't, either."

"Put the cork back," she told him. "You can always drink it later."

"I probably won't."

"I wish you would. It was expensive. It really shouldn't go to waste."

For a time, they sat without speaking. The wind was warm and dry on their faces.

"It will be high enough." She wasn't asking a question.

"I think it will."

"I'm not the first here."

"No, you're not."

"You need to make sure. Afterward."

"As usual, you've thought of everything."

"It's what I do," she smiled.

"I need you."

"You don't. You never really have. And now you have the chance to stop pretending you do."

Ruby handed Colin her glass. It was still half full. She stood. Then he stood. They kissed. She held on to him tightly. He was still holding both glasses.

"I want you to kiss Tony when you see him," she told him, "and I want you to make it very soon."

He couldn't speak. All he could do was not hold her properly and nod his head.

"I have always loved you, Colin Tugdale."

She pulled away from him, took the glasses from his hands, and placed them on the bench.

He put his head in his hands and sobbed.

She lifted his head up, and she looked into his eyes. "You really shouldn't cry."

"I know," he whispered, "I'm sorry."

She let go of him, smiled, and turned away. Ruby Tugdale took one step toward the edge of the cliff. She paused. For a moment it seemed to him as if she might reconsider. But she didn't. She ran. And then she leaped, as far as she could.

It was a moment before Colin sat down on the bench. He lifted up the two glasses. He considered his options. He could drink all the wine . . . some of the wine . . . or none of the wine. Or he could run and jump, and he could die.

In the end, Colin Tugdale carefully poured the rest of the wine onto the grass. The dark red stain lasted only a moment on the dry, sandy ground.

Before he placed the wine bottle and the two glasses safely back inside the backpack and began his walk back, Colin Tugdale had something to do. He needed to be sure.

Part of the weld was some kind of monitor, so that when you concluded, they knew. He found his phone in the front pocket of his trousers. He opened a link to the government website, and from there he was prompted to enter his wife's name and her Social Security number.

The wait time was minimal. The message, when it arrived, was equally brief. According to very recently updated government records, Ruby Margaret Tugdale had concluded.

He started to walk. As he did so, he kept telling himself that he loved to walk.

The number was two-three-eight-one.

He felt guilty that he hadn't looked down at the water afterwards. He couldn't. Did he start to cry again? Or had he been crying the whole time?

The number was two-three-eight-one.

It was without question the worst walk of his life. And Colin Tugdale loved to walk.

The number was two-three-eight-one.

JUSTIN

He should have been suspicious when he saw the parking lot. As he turned off his engine, the last of the pre-dawn darkness lingered over the Chester industrial park. The night shift at the vegetable packing factory that shared the newspaper's lot had just ended, and the giant freezers were being de-iced by a skeleton crew before the day shift arrived.

But even so, there were far fewer cars than usual.

There was a gentle drizzle at the start of Justin Everly's last full day in Chester. That seemed about right. When he recalled his life there, the accompanying soundtrack would feature rain hitting the roof of his car as he drove aimlessly, puddles forming on worn road surfaces, and wet paper blown into the doorways of long-shuttered stores and businesses in the ruin of downtown.

While Justin had often imagined both the day and the details precipitating his departure, it was on this particular day that the twin blows came one after the other, with enough impact to force his hand. As a result, by the end of the work day, his mind would be made up. And by the start of the next day, Justin Everly would be leaving town.

The first blow would be delivered face to face, in the foreboding emptiness of the lot, as the rain slicked up the sidewalk outside the offices of the *Chester Clarion.*

"You could have texted me. To let me know. Let me sleep a little longer."

"Yeah . . . well . . . you know. We just found out about it ourselves. It all happened fast. Last night. There was an emergency staff meeting. The big bosses showed up. That was when they told us."

"The paper's going to be closing?"

"Oh no. Not closing. But the print version is done. The daily print edition. Effective immediately, they said. It'll be online only from now on. Less staff for them to pay. Less overhead. Less production costs."

"And you sure don't need me to deliver it anymore."

It wasn't a question; he just said it to have the last word.

The news hadn't been all that surprising. The *Clarion* was failing because the town was failing. Justin was the oldest driver for the newspaper. The others were all college kids earning some extra money before their morning classes began. They each worked only a couple of the weekday shifts.

But Justin Everly had been the full seven-day man, including the big edition on Sundays, when he had the job all to himself, when delivering it took up most of his morning.

∞

Five minutes later Justin got into his car and started to drive home in the rain.

It was early, and still dark.

Justin lived in an apartment complex halfway between Chester and Lawrence. It was normally a short drive, one that barely gave him long enough to somberly consider that Chester was a world-class toilet of a town.

He had delivered the last print gasps of the once-proud *Clarion* for the past three years. He'd gotten the job right after his three years of junior college. He had changed his major three times and never gotten any closer to graduation. By the end of his third year, his grades were finally respectable. His last stated major was Video Game Design, his fellow classmates a collection of mostly directionless slackers. Justin was the star of the class, but by year three his money had run out, and the only scholarships available at Lawrence Community were from long-distance haulage companies looking to hire fresh drivers and insomniacs.

Three majors. Three years of college.

After abandoning college, Justin had cobbled together a sad trio of jobs to keep afloat. He had needed all three to come up with his share of rent and utilities and the cable/ internet bill, since the option to move back in with his parents was not worthy of serious consideration.

He now had two roommates, plus himself (there was that three deal happening again), in a decent-sized third-floor place halfway between Lawrence, where the college was, and Chester, where he grew up, where he now worked, and where his methed-out parents partied with their sad-sack neighbors, each taking turns to manufacture and share the homegrown pharmaceutical product that had earned Chester notoriety in a big-city newspaper article (not the *Clarion*) published just last week. The subject had been the unlikely juxtaposition of dirt-cheap narcotics and serious graft in rural crapholes where civilized Sunday-newspaper-reading folks couldn't quite bring themselves to believe that big money could be mined. But rural grafters like Larry Charlton, the combination mayor, drug lord, number-one self-serving pimp, and hospital board chair, proved the urbane city slickers wrong, by making his fortune, by avoiding both litigation and publicity, taking the sorry substrata of Chester by their scrawny necks and running them through a wringer that squeezed every last drop of money out of them.

What was rare about this particular newspaper article was that Larry Charlton was specifically identified.

What wasn't rare was that the reporter managed to include the nicknames of Lawrence ("Larry") and Chester ("Chet") that the local folks liked to use, or that what was arguably Larry's (the person, that is) most audacious piece of scamming wasn't even mentioned.

It never was. Maybe it was too hard to believe. Because for sheer balls-out audacity, this was far and away his coup de grâce. Larry Charlton sold illegal Genewelds to the townspeople of Chester for a neighborly twenty grand a weld.

It worked like this: The local hospital where Larry served faithfully on the board did regular scans for the regular folks and regular welds for the regular fifty-five-year-olds who passed the regular scan. Nothing remotely shady there. The regulars passed, or they failed, legitimately. They were paid legitimately by the government for the weld. And they lived their twenty more years in the usual medical stasis, and then they quietly up and croaked. Larry made the square root of zero on that avenue of business.

But on the side, Larry offered the weld for his personal clientele base; specifically, for young and wasted losers under fifty-five and long-addicted scan failures over fifty-five, but in truth for anyone desperate, for whom twenty thousand was going to both be a stretch and a final prayer in a life fast running out of prayers.

Larry didn't bother to offer the option of the scan. There was no need. It didn't matter if they passed or failed the scan.

They would all be welded. As long as they paid Larry cash. And then they were required to keep quiet.

Larry was not the world's only illegal welder. There were constant media reports of shady weld practices (a favorite name for it was "scan scam") that ranged from small-time all the way up to government-controlled. In third world countries, Larrys were legion. Most were ultimately exposed. Larry Charlton doubtless would be too. But for now, he operated under a rigid code of silence. It was firmly understood that if he were to be exposed, the toxic underbelly of Chester would lose its last hope.

In Larry's secret world, there were two forms of addict, and the weld worked either one or two kinds of magic on them. If you were young and your health was good (except for the meth or the opioids or whatever other addiction you had selected), and you might have passed the scan, you scored a double break. Your system got a full detoxing reboot (known as a ScanClense), so that, if you somehow managed to never do any more meth or heroin, or you stopped drinking cheap whisky for breakfast, you bought yourself a sporting chance at twenty years of looking good and feeling fine.

That was the better of the two options, even if you only lived another twenty years.

And then there was the second-best option, the one for post-scan addicts defined as genetically bad, the kind of bad that failed the scan. But there was still the cleansing/detoxing benefit to be had, so that even the most pathetic junkie could still catch a break.

For the addict with other health-related issues, the weld still generated a complete detoxification of your system, without the inconvenience of harrowing withdrawal, without pious rituals of repentance, or long nights of sweat-soaked, shuddering agony.

Justin's parents had used up the last of his college money to pay for their welds. It cost them forty grand they didn't have, and there was no twofer discount offered. Justin had carefully saved his money, and his grandparents, when they had both been alive, had dutifully chipped in. He could probably have attended the big state college up north for two years or so with his funds. He was pretty smart, and his grades in high school were good enough for some form of partial scholarship.

But his money was long gone.

And, after their respective welds, his folks were still unrepentant junkies.

While it was still early, the sun had grudgingly pulled itself up and over dying downtown Chester as Justin Everly, only son of welded addicts, onetime community college student, and former newspaper delivery boy, maneuvered his small car through an assault course of potholed roadway. Justin had finished making the payments on his car last month. It had taken him three years. He had paid, when you calculated the interest, almost exactly one-third more than the asking price of the car, and his car was currently worth two-thirds of what it was worth when he first drove it off the lot.

While there was no way to make the math work in his favor, he was proud that he owned the car outright, just as he was cognizant of the fact that, since it was now out of warranty, it would commence breaking down any time now.

So, being both cautious and in no real hurry to get anywhere, he drove through Chester without haste.

The Chester Savings Bank and the Chester Public Library buildings each languished on the two diagonal corners of the four-way intersection in the center of town.

The two structures were almost identical, with hunched grey angel sculptures perched aloft on all four corners.

Both were constructed simultaneously, boldly imagined by architect Sebastian Merry, commissioned by the Chester Chamber of Commerce a century ago, back in the days when the industrial heart of the state was still pumping money.

Merry was commissioned to design a number of institutions in the heartland.

A half century after his demise, Sebastian Merry would be declared an architectural icon and a visionary of pre-modernist sensibility, although neither attribute would generate one thin dime for Chester, or for the preservation of the two pigeon-shit-splattered buildings that sulked in the wasteland of downtown Chester.

At the doughnut shop, twin tattooed ladies served Justin his large coffee and Boston creme in a blur of efficiency. As always, he thanked them. As always, they were reluctant to speak. It was the only place in town that was open in the early hours when he started delivering the *Clarion*.

Back at the apartment everything had changed. Three weeks ago, his two roommates had simultaneously acquired new girlfriends, in a revolutionary development. Both roommates were, much like Justin, bashful creatures possessed of no social skills. They had questionable wardrobes. They played computer games and ate fast food at all hours. Neither could be referred to as a catch. Yet, there they were. Caught.

While neither young lady would stand to win any beauty contest, they were several echelons above the slack-jawed, knuckle-dragging cave trolls that Justin would have expected his gormless roomies to have rustled up. The boys were punching well above their weight.

And Justin was just as baffled as they were.

Both ladies regularly slept over. While they had not previously known each other, they had instantly bonded. Most mornings, they were in the kitchen, boisterous, giggly, the dual creators of elaborate if culinarily pedestrian breakfasts for their two slumbering sweeties.

On most sleepover occasions, Justin was careful to be out of the apartment long before the chefs arose, but on occasional days off, he would lie trapped in his bedroom, groaning deep inside himself.

This morning, Justin was enthusiastically welcomed. He was offered something hot, freshly made.

Thank God he could truthfully say that, after his sizable doughnut, he wasn't hungry. He muttered a polite demurral and skedaddled to his room, where he hastily shut the thin wood veneer door.

Inside his sanctuary, Justin sought to soothe his troubled mind by playing Trench Warfare on his homemade computer for just as long as it would take the chatty cooks and their pampered menfolk to devour the fruits of the women's labor.

He could hear vague stirrings from the other two bedrooms. The aroma of freshly cooked vittles had roused the gentlemen.

He tried harder to relax.

Justin's roomies were likeable enough. And they had always seemed to like Justin just fine. But now they both had girlfriends who were around a lot, and Justin had sensed that an awkward conversation over next year's apartment lease was forthcoming. Three days ago, he had been asked in a studiedly casual manner if he was still intending to stay next year. He had said that he wasn't sure. He would let them know. They said okay. That it was cool. They said whatever. All three names were on the lease. Their landlord was easy going.

Justin could see where this was going. In three months, he would need to find another place to live. And now he was down one source of income.

He didn't blame the boys one bit. He liked his roommates. Their girlfriends were okay. They all had jobs that paid more than Justin made. Splitting the rent four ways would be easy. Obviously the boys would want the girls to move in and Justin to move out. They were lucky. They had partners. He wasn't lucky. He didn't.

The relaxing wasn't going as well as he had hoped.

Justin would need another strategy.

On his hands and knees, Justin pulled a folded piece of paper out from under the bed. He sat on top of the blanket and spread the paper out in front of him.

Justin spent long hours staring at his map. While there was no large body of water or identifying outline of coastline, a multitude of small lakes dotted the landscape. There were no towns and few roads. Dashed lines ran from one lake to the next. The word *lake* was abbreviated *Lk*. The dashed lines had numbers attached to them. And the suffix *r*, which stood for *rods*. One dashed line connected Glass Lk to Fellowship Lk. It measured 67r. Small black triangles littered the edges of the lakes. Some of the triangles had been filled in with a highlighter. The highlighted triangles were often adorned with a checkmark. Justin had added a number of blue lines linking one lake to another; several lines had also been traced over with red or green highlighter. There was a compass rose near the bottom right corner and, beside it, a scale with a ratio of inches to miles. Two formulas converted rods to feet and rods to miles. Each rod was 16.5 feet. Each mile was 320 rods.

At the very bottom of the map, Justin had added a key to his own modifications.

YELLOW TRIANGLE = *stayed there*
YELLOW TRIANGLE WITH CHECKMARK = *nice site*
BLUE LINE = *walking trail*
GREEN DASHED LINE = *easy*
RED DASHED LINE = *hard*

For some people, relaxation took two aspirins or a dry martini, a series of deep breathing exercises, a half hour of yoga, or an episode of a soap opera. Justin sat and studied his map for as long as it took for him to unwind. When he was done, mentally and physically relaxed, only then was he ready to engage the Hun at the First Battle of Ypres in the world of Trench Warfare.

In the real world, the first battle for the Belgian town had been an inconclusive affair resulting in one hundred thousand casualties.

The Germans had unleashed poison gas for the first time at the Second Battle of Ypres, but this was of little concern to Justin; he was still engaged in the first skirmish, and he had earned enough online credits for the mask upgrade.

Ready for battle, General Justin Everly waited expectantly in his muddy trench. He had read several accounts of the real wartime battles. He knew that the period poets spoke of the poignant pause of stillness, as the circling birds fell silent, as a collective intake of breath preceded the start of each historic offensive.

Justin made sure his rifle was loaded and his bayonet was attached. He was determined to go over the top with his men. He had arranged for artillery support. There would be shrapnel fire distracting the enemy when he and his soldiers made their push. He had carefully chosen positions for his snipers.

He was ready.

∞

Later in the morning, fresh from battle, Justin Everly arrived at the Tidy Diner for his second job.

The main road south out of Chester was the chosen location for the smattering of businesses determined to crawl clear of the socioeconomic death throes gripping the town center. Two fast-food franchises duked it out for the teenage trade. There was a liquor store with an enviable selection of expensive malt whiskies, a thrift shop affiliated with a local church, and an auto parts company sharing space with a muffler repair shop.

Tidy Diner, owned by the Bob Tidy family, was open six days a week, serving breakfast and lunch on weekdays and breakfast only on Saturdays. During the week, the Tidy catered to local patrons in the early morning hours and to transient trade in the afternoon, from people in cars anxious to eat cheaply and well, and to spend as little time as possible in Chester.

Bob Tidy permanently sat vigil at the register, which was positioned near the front door. Most of his customers swore they'd never seen Bob anyplace else. Bob was a huge bear of a man. He wore massive shorts and equally voluminous T-shirts year-round, with tall white compression socks pulled all the way up to his pale, formless knees. His seat was a high stool, on which he half sat and half leaned, his walker and a walking stick positioned close by.

Bob looked unhealthy. He was perpetually sweaty, and his color fluctuated between beet-red and corpse-white.

Bob Tidy was still six years away from his scan, and he did not expect it to go well. While much of what ailed him was technically treatable, the congenital heart disease inherited from past generations of Tidy men was not. By his own reckoning, Bob would die the natural way, and the amount of money he anticipated spending on keeping his wreck of a carcass intact kept him awake at night as regularly as his acid reflux.

While Bob lay awake in the early hours, his wife, Elma, who was reported to be skeletally thin and a model of robust health, made pies in the kitchen of their nearby house. She rarely set foot inside the diner.

The three Ruiz brothers manned the counter and the kitchen and helped Bob and Elma's daughter, Avril, wait on tables when she was overwhelmed, which tended to happen the most during lunchtimes.

When the Tidy Diner needed one more pair of hands, Justin worked the lunch shift, five days a week, loading the dishwasher, unloading the dishwasher, making pot after pot of weak yet stewed coffee, then pouring cup after cup of the cursed beverage, wiping down the tables, setting the tables, sweeping the floors, and all the while languishing in love unrequited, for the fair Avril, who was blissfully unaware of her effect on the romantically stunted Justin.

It was the customer closest to the front door who would deliver the four words that would precipitate the second blow of the day to Justin, who was still recovering from his earlier loss of income, but whose plucky British Expeditionary Force had held the young and inexperienced German army at bay earlier this morning, incurring only the most limited of casualties during the hostilities.

"Avril's going to college."

As with the downsizing of the *Clarion*, this second piece of news wasn't earth-shattering. Avril Tidy was smart and ready for college. She was already two years out of high school and had worked in the diner to help her parents. She had done well on a battery of aptitude tests and written the requisite essays. Some scholarship money was forthcoming. It wasn't going to be quite enough, but it would have to do.

"Who's going to work the diner?" Justin managed to choke out.

"The Ruiz boys have a little sister."

This was news to Justin.

It was still early in the summer.

In a daze, he washed his hands and found a clean apron. The dirty dishes were stacked on the counter beside the dishwasher as he started to fill the gullet of the industrial-size machine.

He'd lost a low-paying job that he hated and needed in equal measure. He'd lost the girl he had never really possessed in the first place. On the plus side, he'd managed to hold the might of the empire-thirsting German army at bay.

On balance, it wasn't nearly enough.

At the end of the shift, he collected his paycheck from Bob and said his goodbyes to Avril and the Ruiz brothers. Their sister showed up, and Justin forced a smile and made himself say hello. Gabby was perky and cute, and everyone in the diner would love her and quickly forget about Avril, and Justin decided to hate her on principle. Today was Friday. She would start on Monday. Bob and Elma were throwing a party in the diner on Sunday evening to say goodbye to Avril who was going to stay with an aunt out east and then come back for a few days before heading off to college.

Justin stood by as Avril and Gabby bonded. Avril told her who the worst tippers and the best customers were. Gabby wanted to know what it was like to work with her three horrible brothers. Avril said she loved them all and would miss them, and Gabby snorted a response, but they both kept laughing.

As the customers paid their bills, Bob stopped a few favorites to invite them to say goodbye to Avril on Sunday. Avril told her father not to spend too much money on the party. She would need a car. The campus was not easy to get around. She wanted to come home as often as she could. The bus service to Chester was terrible. There was no direct train.

Her father looked pained at the mention of a car, and he shook his head.

Someone asked whether Bob's wife, Elma, would be there on Sunday. Bob said he wasn't sure, but she had promised her husband her finest pies.

Bob said that he would miss having Avril around and that Chester sure was a hell of a mess, and no one argued either point with him.

Avril gave everyone big hugs and said that she would miss them all.

Under normal circumstances, Justin would have been able to convince himself that her eyes lingered the longest on him as she spoke. But these were not normal circumstances. Justin was suddenly aware that he had spent too much time manufacturing subliminal flirtations.

Justin was opening the front door of the diner when Avril asked, "Are you coming? On Sunday?"

"I'll try to," he lied.

"I won't see you tomorrow."

"No," he said. Justin didn't work on Saturdays.

"I don't know why we open. It's only breakfast. Hardly anyone comes in. I think Dad does it for the regulars."

"What will you study?"

"I'm undeclared. I didn't know when I applied. Now I want to do something with the environment. Nature. Conservation. Some biology. But not too much regular science. More like earth science. Wildlife. Marine life. Animals." She laughed at herself. "I'm all over the place."

It had taken him until now, until she was leaving, to find out that she liked the things he liked.

He tried to imagine her as a marine biologist. It wasn't hard.

"So maybe undeclared is best for you right now."

"I think so." She changed the subject. "You went."

"Just junior college."

"Still college," she said. "You should go back."

Justin smiled at her. "Money."

"Tell me about it."

Justin grew scared of what he might blurt out next. So, he left.

∞

The remaining third of Justin's trifecta of unskilled servitude was his sporadic evening shift as barback and occasional bartender at the Dripping Tap, formerly known as Sandy's Tap. After Sandy died, the current owner, Andy, bought the place in cash with money his dad had given him. Andy wanted to rename it after himself but the names were too close, and Andy worried that customers might be confused.

Andy's dad was none other than Larry Charlton, weldmaster and the nearest thing to a criminal mastermind in Chester. Despite his lineage, Andy Charlton was well liked. He was never stumbling drunk and never sober and uptight; instead, he was always half hammered. He enjoyed early morning shots with the delivery guys to get the day started. A half-consumed glass of beer was a fixture on a shelf behind the bar, where Andy would stand and half help out if and when the place got busy.

All employees were allocated two shift drinks, but Andy never kept count. At the end of the night, two became four, with shots on the side. When everyone tried to stumble out into the parking lot behind the bar at the first sign of morning, Andy intervened, paying for cabs home out of his own pocket.

Andy always stayed until closing, and after. Sitting at the far end of the bar, with the last of his half beers in front of him.

The next morning, Andy was there first. The first half beer tapped. If there had been a delivery, he would have done his first couple of shots already.

Did he ever leave? Or did he just put his head down on the bar counter for a couple of hours between the last shift drink and the morning beer truck?

No one was sure. His clothes looked the same. But there was a box filled with bar T-shirts that everyone took and wore. He never looked like he had shaved.

Justin usually worked three nights a week. He wasn't much of a bartender, because he wasn't much of a drinker, and his lack of interest in the subject matter showed. He was paid less than minimum wage, and, since he was employed mostly as a barback, the reverse pyramid of tip money left him at the short end of the financial stick. Some weeks he did better than others. A handful of the bar staff liked him, and he made more on the evenings when he worked with them. Between his three jobs, Justin survived, but most of the staff only worked at the Tap, and they didn't make enough to get by.

It helped that Andy was known to offer cash advances that he didn't always remember to collect.

A lot of people in town wondered how Larry Charlton put up with Andy. But the Tap was the nicest bar in a shitty town full of sad people, so it couldn't help but make money. Most people figured that the senior Charlton was in for a major cut.

Larry seldom entered the place. When he did, it was usually very late at night, near closing time. His face always darkened as he looked around.

Justin dried glasses and watched Larry.

Larry Charlton studied the bar, like he was calculating all the ways Andy was not making money properly. Not watering down the drinks enough. Not allowing hopeless drunks to get drunker and run up easily padded bar tabs. Not dealing drugs in the bar when the place was rife with hapless suckers.

Larry always drank a whisky-and-honey liqueur that the bar was obliged to stock, even though no one else drank it. He never had more than two. He sat at a table alone. If all the tables were occupied, he would wait for one to clear. The bar staff knew that Larry was to be given a heavy pour and was not to be presented with a bill. He was also not expected to tip.

Against the downward momentum of the day, Justin had a good night. The bar was packed, and the staff were slammed. Everyone served and bussed, and the tips peaked as the nearest big college basketball team triumphed in an overtime buzzer-beater. Andy bought a round of shots for the whole bar.

At the end of the night, Justin picked up his paycheck, which he signed over for cash, and two hundred more in tips for the night, mostly in ones and fives.

Justin passed on the shift drinks, as he usually did. Andy patted him on the shoulder as he slipped him another fifty in fives and tens. Justin left the bar a half hour after closing time and drove home. He stopped at an ATM to deposit his diner paycheck. Andy would have cashed that for him, too. He hadn't thought to ask.

At the start of the evening the Tap had been quiet, and Justin was able to do some calculating. He had three more rent payments to make. They were automatic withdrawals from his account. After that, the lease was up. He calculated his share of the utilities. The three roomies shared internet/cable services. He was good for one-third of that amount.

When he finished calculating his liabilities, he took what was left out of his checking account. It came to around two grand. There was another seven hundred in his wallet. Another three hundred in the apartment.

∞

The apartment was quiet when he got home. Both sets of loving couples had retired much earlier.

Justin canceled his phone service. He had prepaid for the month and had a small credit coming. He wrote a check for everything he could think of that would come due and left it on the kitchen table where his roommates would find it. He thought he might be short. His furniture and his clothes were worthless. His computer was the best one in the apartment. They could keep it or cannibalize it for parts. He thought that might be enough to settle his account.

Finally, he found the car title and signed it over to Avril Tidy. She had said she would need a car at college. He left that on the kitchen table as well. His roommates would take it to the Tidy Diner for him.

He was sorry to be missing the party for Avril. The pies would be excellent.

He pulled his money out of his packets and spread it on the table. Under normal circumstances it wouldn't last him long. But these were not normal circumstances. He would make it last as long as he could.

He was leaving town in the morning.

COLIN

In the grief-wracked days that followed, Colin Tugdale puttered aimlessly around his home in the city. He thought often about his concluded wife. But it seemed to him that he spent almost as much time thinking about the four numbers on the lock; about two, and three, and eight, and one.

The lock was purely tactile and talismanic. He sat at his kitchen table. He drank his coffee. He held the lock in one hand. He put his coffee cup down to open it, to close it, and then to open it again.

When he thought about his wife it was hard to keep away from the end. When he did think about her conclusion, it was to reflect upon the fact that, as always, she had managed to think of everything.

Colin Tugdale had returned to their house in the city three days after her death. In what was once the cozy clutter of the family room, almost all of his late wife's books were gone, pulled down from the shelves, boxed and abandoned in a series of waterproof containers outside a local resale shop, along with her tiny cache of newer, fancier clothing. Ruby had insisted on doing this task herself.

He found one remaining cardboard box of her newest books. She had used a blue marker to write an address on the top, and Colin had dutifully driven there.

The city boasted numerous little free libraries—pretty wooden cases, brightly painted, for the housing and trading of books. This particular one was clearly brand new. Colin carefully placed the titles inside. He noticed that some of the books were also brand new. They were unread. Some were children's books. Some were written by authors he knew Ruby had little time for, and he could only surmise that she had chosen the contents of her little library with others in mind.

Now as he glanced at the mostly empty shelves, he saw that there were a few other books that she had left behind, stories he recalled her telling him about over the years, stories she thought he might like. She had carefully arranged the few volumes that remained, cleaning the shelves, artfully spreading out the knickknacks, trying to make the gaps in the collection as inconspicuous as possible. It had been a noble but unsuccessful endeavor.

Colin told himself he would commence his new reading life very soon.

She had left one item in their bedroom closet, a garment he had long assumed to be her old college sweatshirt. Ruby had been a member of the field hockey team.

Colin had asked her to leave it there when she packed up her things.

He recalled that it had languished there forever, before Colin had accidentally knocked it from a hanger one morning. When he had picked it up, he was surprised at how large it was. He tried it on. It fit perfectly. It was much too large for his wife because, as she finally admitted, it had been purchased as a gift for a college boyfriend, or would-be college boyfriend, a bashful young gentleman who had looked panic stricken when she presented him with this token of an affection he was unwilling to reciprocate.

"So, you got me instead." He was smiling as he spoke.

She smiled back, "It would seem so."

"Don't I get the sweatshirt now?" he asked playfully.

She shook her head. "You don't ever wear sweatshirts."

"Was he the sweatshirt type?"

"I thought so."

Ruby let him keep the sweatshirt.

In the years that followed, Colin wore the sweatshirt on occasion. His wife's name had been Jarvis, which was silk-screened on the back, along with her number, which was 59. Ruby Jarvis had played all four years of college, mostly in the midfield. She had loved field hockey.

Ruby had placed the rest of her regular clothes, the casual things she wore most days, in a box on the garage floor. He moved it up onto a high shelf when she declared the collection much too threadbare for even the bargain racks at the Goodwill. He hadn't argued with her.

When he returned to the house, after her conclusion, Colin decided that the box would go out on the very next garbage day. He had told himself that. He had been quite firm. That had been yesterday morning. The box was still in the garage. He had now hoisted it high up in the rafters.

Two days before the trip east, they had argued over a framed poster, one she somehow knew he had long disliked. She told him it should go. But Colin had uncharacteristically dug in his heels. It was still on the dining room wall. And it would stay there. He had won that particular battle. Even if he did hate it.

They had sold her car to a local man with a teenage daughter. It was new, with few miles, and it was well maintained. Ruby told him to put the money toward replacing his car. His car was older, she reasoned, and much too fast, and it slurped gasoline hungrily and lacked most of the latest safety features. But he had refused. The car money had been dropped into their bank account, which was already too swollen for him to ever find the time to spend in the year and a half that remained for him.

The Tugdales owed next to nothing to anyone. Their small house in the city was paid for long ago. They had considered buying a cottage up north, on a small lake surrounded by other small lakes. But then Tony had up and done that for them, picking the location well, then handing over the keys unexpectedly one sunny afternoon. It was a six-hour drive, even in Colin's fast car, crossing three state lines, actually re-crossing one line. It was in a stark and beautiful place, alluringly desolate in the short blink of summer, dauntingly desolate and frozen in the extended haul of the winter. They had made their son promise to share it with them.

Tony Tugdale had dutifully smiled and agreed, but he had seldom made it up there.

Colin and Ruby, especially Ruby, had adored the place, as much for itself as for the fact that their clever son had given it to them.

Just prior to her conclusion, Ruby had made a last solo trip north to the cottage, where she had carefully siphoned her existence out. It would be fair to say that Ruby Tugdale had sponged her life away, as much as she was able, and in the immediate aftermath of her conclusion, the government had seen to the few areas she had been forced to leave unwiped.

"Can you please verify the location of your wife's conclusion, Mr. Tugdale?" The woman had said her name was Eloise at the beginning of the call.

He spoke slowly. His voice wasn't steady. "We had gone for a walk along the cliffs. On the edge of town." Then he added pointlessly, "it was beside the water."

"I see." Eloise spoke, and Colin could hear her type simultaneously.

Calling the department was just a courtesy. All welded people were monitored. Colin knew that Ruby's death had already been recorded, had been recorded seconds after it occurred. He had already used his phone, visited the department website, and confirmed Ruby's conclusion, all in a matter of minutes after she was gone. But for the sake of form, Colin was calling this in, as the Department of Conclusions required. More importantly, Ruby had told him to make the official call.

There was a lengthy pause before Eloise spoke again. "Your wife has already been located and we can confirm her successful conclusion. You have the department's sympathies at this time, Mr. Tugdale. All our records have been amended. I can also confirm that our staff are on their way. Will it be a ground burial, a cremation, or a more specialized method of disposition?"

The department already knew this, but Colin told Eloise that it would be a cremation. There was more typing. Eloise told him that the government would be able to arrange this for him, if he still so desired. He told Eloise that he did indeed so desire. Ruby had been very clear about her cremation.

Colin's thoughts on her chosen method of disposal strayed at that point. But Eloise gently reeled him back in. She still needed to know where to send the ashes. "You have two addresses currently on file." He confirmed that this was so. Ruby had wanted her ashes to be evenly divided. Some would be spread in the garden of their city house, and the rest would be sprinkled along the edge of the lake up north.

After a moment's thought, Colin Tugdale asked Eloise to ship his wife's ashes to the city. He would, he decided, drive up to the cottage in a week or so.

"Are there articles that need to be returned?"

Colin assured Eloise that there were not. This was an unnecessary consideration. Ruby had thought to remove her wedding ring before she jumped. There would be nothing else. Nothing, that is, but her blood-soiled pieces of clothing, covering her broken body, shattered on the salty wet rocks. Colin began to fall apart at that point in the conversation. It was fortunate that Eloise had no more questions to ask, because Colin could no longer have supplied her with a sentient response.

At the termination of the call, Eloise thanked Colin for calling and, on behalf of the department, she once again tendered a generic sorrow for his loss. After Colin had numbly thanked her for her kindness, he had quickly hung up.

Now Colin was back home, in his small house in the city, where the ashes, as promised, had arrived that morning. Colin had opened the box and extracted the small urn. He had walked across the wet grass in the back garden. As near as he could judge he had poured out half the contents. It was hard to tell. He cried when he started, and he was crying much harder when he finished.

As promised, the department had taken care of everything. After a succinct and factually accurate—if somewhat impersonal—obituary was posted on various sites, Ruby's name, and indeed her very existence, had commenced a gentle rendering. Their joint bank accounts became solely his bank accounts. The few feeble pieces of junk mail and plaintive solicitations they received now came addressed solely to Mr. Colin Tugdale. Colin was never billed for any of the conclusion arrangements. That amount had been factored into the Weld Wad. Ruby was no longer insured to drive his car. Her electronic passwords no longer unlocked anything, her ATM card no longer accessed cash withdrawals. Colin would not have been surprised to find that her front-door key no longer worked. But it did. Between the department and Ruby, her vanishing had been both swift and relentless.

Colin sat at his kitchen table in the reformative light of the early morning.

He had slept badly again. For most of the last decade Colin Tugdale woke up every morning of every day at the exact time he had woken every morning of every workday for the previous three decades, several hours before he had to get to work to troubleshoot the school district's network of computers. On most workdays when the weather was accommodating, he had walked to the administration building from home. Once he was there, he checked the firewalls and filters. He dutifully answered the half-dozen emails he received each morning. One of the teachers would usually wonder why the research sites he or she tried to access for his or her master's thesis were always blocked. He told him or her that IT policy was handled by the superintendent, Dr. Matt Currie, who Colin disliked, if only because Dr. Matt Currie had seen fit to dislike Colin first. He would usually have to advise at least two teachers who couldn't access the district website to turn off and reboot their computers before they filled out the requisite technology work order form.

When he had finished with his routine morning e-correspondence, Colin usually had time on his hands. Often, he emailed his son, who would not answer until later in the day. Sometimes he pulled up maps of potential walking trips for his two summer months. These he would stare at longingly.

Now Colin Tugdale sat in his kitchen with half his dead wife's ashes in a container, an open padlock in his hand, and an empty coffee cup on the table.

∞

After he returned home from his final trip with Ruby, Colin was unable to resist. He played the numbers.

His initial strategy had been to buy several lottery tickets incorporating all four numbers. Which he did. He never once won big. He never once even came close to winning big. One time his ticket yielded a thirty-dollar payout. He was slightly amused when this happened. He wasn't especially looking to make money.

Next, Colin took to walking the streets of the city alone. If he thought no one was watching, he compulsively twisted bicycle locks as he walked past. There were always commuter bikes chained up beside the nearest transit station, the brick-walled ambiance of the coffee shop, the two competing corner bars offering a strict diet of artisan beverages, and the LGBTQ-friendly church with a grim Gothic exterior and a young congregation. Outside each establishment, he hurriedly turned the assembled locks to the same four numbers. But they never once opened for him.

Inside the vestibule of the train station stood one wall of rental storage lockers. They were all accessed by four-digit combination padlocks. The temptation was almost more than he could endure, but every time Colin entered the station there was a security guard standing close by, and he couldn't try his magical combination.

Finally, on a rainy morning, Colin asked the attendant if he could rent a locker for the day. He paid the nominal charge and feebly waved his empty backpack convincingly in the man's face. He was asked which locker he wanted. Colin wasn't ready for the question. There were four rows of lockers. There were ten lockers in each row. The lockers were numbered one through forty.

Colin stared at the lockers and waited for inspiration. With a shrug, he told the gentleman to give him any locker. He was promptly assigned locker number thirty-one. Two of his four numbers, he silently noted.

Colin was handed a gold lock and a folded piece of paper with a four-digit combination: six-nine-one-one. He silently sifted the numbers around in his head for a moment, but he couldn't make them mean anything.

He dialed the numbers, pulled the lock free, opened the empty locker, and shamefacedly placed his empty backpack inside. He noted that the attendant and the security guard could barely be bothered to observe him. The whole process left him feeling foolish.

When he returned later that day to retrieve his backpack, the security guard was miraculously gone. The attendant had deserted his tiny cubicle and was outside the station, talking on his phone, his back to Colin.

Here was his chance. Colin had time to try his numbers

on four of the padlocks. He randomly picked one on each row. None opened. The ticket collector quickly finished his call and returned to his post as grieving weld widower and crack amateur numerologist Colin Tugdale made himself scarce.

One evening he wrote and ran a rudimentary computer program that scrambled and rearranged the numbers into parts of phone numbers and street addresses, into old-fashioned radio station call numbers, into map coordinates, into pretty much anything. Nothing he found had any particular significance. An occult website promised to study the numbers and unearth their hidden spiritual importance. But his four numbers, despite the site's insistence on draping the digits in tones of portentous inference, were quickly revealed to be pedestrian.

Once, to assure himself that madness was not rapidly encroaching, Colin calculated the odds of his having rightly surmised the lock combination in the first place. He was reassured by the sizable number of digits his answer contained.

Because of his job, Colin was more than proficient with computers. Because he was skilled at preventing students from visiting inappropriate websites, he was himself particularly adept at finding appropriate websites. He studied birth dates, death notices, even celestial charts. He placed the four digits in deliberately wide searches and came up with an immense collection of nothing.

Two-three-eight-one. Two-three-eight-one. Two-three-eight-one.

As Colin continued his search, he had a thought. What, he wondered, had occurred on the date two-three-eight-one—as in February third? In 1981? In 1881? In 1781? In 1681?

In no particular order, he received his answers. A fistfight in a rugby stadium becomes the origin of a popular drinking song. A movie actress dies in a car crash minutes after giving birth in the backseat. The baby lives. An obscure act of Parliament all but sanctions child labor. An oil painting signed and dated that very day, month, and year is discovered in a hut halfway across the world and is sold at auction to provide an impoverished village with drinking water. A man born that day out of wedlock in a cave in a cold northern country grows up to become a martyr and a canonized saint, in that order. All prove to be events of interest to someone. But not Colin Tugdale.

∞

After his wife's pre-conclusion, Colin had sat in the crowded terminal and tried to read the first line of the newspaper article for the third time. The flight west was solidly overbooked. Colin already possessed his ticket. Three young children howled at each other in the row behind him.

He was listening with mounting interest to a series of announcements. There were several seats available in first class. The cost to upgrade was in freefall, currently standing at half the usual cost of an upgrade; a conventionally expensive seat, as opposed to a bracingly exorbitant one.

He hesitated. He considered. He eyed the three urchins reproachfully. Still, he was reluctant.

This expenditure seemed out of character. So, was it plausible that this anomaly could be attributed to his very recent loss?

Colin was perplexed. But then, as he thought his way back through the years, to arrive at the very beginning of his fifty-year marriage, it was clear. He hadn't always been thrifty. Ruby was the penny pincher.

Oh, for God's sake, Tugdale, he silently implored. Be honest with yourself. Ruby wasn't frugal. Ruby was downright cheap. And he had loved her in all her parsimony.

The airline employee at the gate made one more frantic plea. The price of an upgrade to first class now stood at one third of the usual price.

So, well aware of the tidy sum to his name in the bank and the short time left to spend it, Colin Tugdale strode purposefully forward. He asked if the noisy trio of youngsters was traveling economy today, and, with that confirmed, he was more than ready to subject himself to some long-overdue pampering.

Affecting the air of a man accustomed to parting with considerable resources in substantial torrents, the freshly weld widowed Colin Tugdale snapped his credit card onto the counter. A crisp shirt sleeve gestured toward the spongy red carpet.

But as he turned in the designated direction, Colin was discreetly summoned back to the counter. The clerk entered his details into the computer for a second time. And in a moment, she had good news. His very recent bereavement had shown up in the airline records, and he was thus declared eligible for an additional funeral discount. Colin explained that there was not going to be a funeral, but was quickly assured that flights undertaken within an allotted time after the death of a concluding spouse were automatically subject to the discounted rate.

So, not only was Colin Tugdale flying high; he was flying high and saving big.

The flight west was three hours long, and the complimentary red wine was better than the respectable vintage with which he had toasted his wife's last living moments. His guilt lessened as he accepted each near-overflowing glassful.

As the plane prepared to land, Colin was handed a thin plastic card and a small piece of paper. The card bore the logo of the airline and the words *rewards suite* embossed on the front. The paper had four numbers written by hand in dark blue ink. Colin glanced down. To his surprise the first two numbers were a two and a three. He held his breath just long enough to register that the third number was another three, while the fourth, as if it even mattered by that point, was a seven.

In his semi-inebriated condition, he almost missed the doorway. There was a slot in the wall beside a keypad. Colin inserted the plastic card into the slot and stubbornly pressed two-three-eight-one. He wasn't too surprised when the red light stayed red and his card slid back out. He pushed the card back in and entered the assigned numbers. Two-three-three-seven. The light turned green and the door opened.

The room was dimly lit and, as far as he could tell, mostly empty. He sat down in the nearest comfortable chair, and he waited. There was the suggestion of acoustic jazz music under a wisp of muted conversation. A waitress wearing a small Celtic cross necklace slid into position, and Colin ordered coffee, which arrived immediately and was truly excellent.

On the plane, he had been told that his rewards benefits, including access to the rewards suite and shuttle service to anywhere in the city, would expire at midnight. There were a great many other services, the steward insinuated. But Colin could sense that the man was reluctant to impart everything. Perhaps he was saving Colin from an overload of intoxicating privilege. He was, after all, only going to be a king for a few hours.

He sat back and sipped his coffee. It came with a thin slice of shortbread that melted on his tongue. The leather seat beneath his rear was rich and soft. In a few minutes, his luggage appeared at his feet, the deliverer retreating too rapidly for Colin to pretend to wrestle with the dilemma of whether or not to tip.

As his eyes adjusted to the darkness, Colin saw a man sitting at a nearby table. He wore a dark blue business suit and a white dress shirt with too many buttons undone. Colin observed a large cigar placed between his fingers, an almost-empty cut glass tumbler on the table, then the flash of a lighter, which lingered for a moment, as the cigar was carefully primed, before the first enveloping mushroom of smoke. Perhaps the smoker prolonged the beloved ritual a shade too long. But just before the smoke cloud arrived, his features were illuminated in profile. The contours of the face were shrouded in more beard and stubble than Colin remembered. And while the remnants of hair on the top of the head were presumably freshly shaved close up against the scalp, Colin was certain that he was getting a glimpse of Mr. Elliot Devine, a prolific acquirer of tech companies who had ventured high and lost gracelessly in a buyout attempt for ownership of Trench Warfare.

Colin remembered the bitterly fought campaign that pitted Mr. Devine against maverick gaming maven Anthony Tugdale, only son of Colin Tugdale, recently weld widowed, and more recently the temporary recipient of international jet-set status.

Seeing Devine was a surprise for Colin. He kept staring into the reconfiguring darkness. Although Colin was usually very good with names and faces, in this instance, there was good reason to be uncertain: Elliot Devine had recently concluded, at the unsurprising age of seventy-five.

Just to be sure, Colin pulled out his phone and searched for his obituary. It didn't take long. Devine was indeed just as dead as Colin had remembered. Colin remembered having read the obituary, which didn't directly mention that Devine had concluded, but had lived to be the exact age of conclusion, and the accompanying photograph, dated close to the time of his death, showed a gentleman in love with the great outdoors and looking to be at most in his mid fifties.

Colin put his phone away and sipped his still-warm drink. He felt it safe to assume that Devine was indeed dead, that he had concluded.

So why then was he firing up a stogie in a chair less than twenty feet from Colin?

The attempted buyout had been a secret deal, involving camouflaged leverage, an enticing promise/mirage of copious stock options, and cursory amounts of cash. Mr. Devine had been haughty in the beginning negotiations, growing increasingly astounded, and then angry, as his offers came up short, and young Mr. Tugdale, heeding the advice of his father and a great many others, opted to keep control of his prize asset.

Tony had met with Devine several times in person. Colin hadn't had the privilege, but he was well aware of what he looked like.

When Colin next looked up, the deceased dealmaker and his cigar were both gone, and his empty glass was no longer sitting on the table.

The rebirth of Elliot Devine was another mystery for Colin Tugdale to consider, as he sat in his kitchen, his morning coffee now mostly cold, and the better part of the day in danger of sneaking away from him.

His day was destined to get stranger.

His phone rang. He glanced at the number on the screen. It was an unfamiliar number; private and local. He answered on the fourth ring.

"Is your wife dead?" It was a woman's voice.

"I beg your pardon."

"Is she dead?"

"Who is this?"

"Just tell me if she's dead or not."

"Yes. She's dead. Who the hell is this?"

"You have my condolences."

"What?"

"I'm sorry she's dead."

"Who are you?"

"You'll soon find out. I'll be right over."

The call ended.

JUSTIN

If you had asked Justin Everly which summer had been his finest, he might initially have sneered and informed you that they all sucked. But that would have been disingenuous. If you had persisted, he would have conceded that he remembered his fifteenth one most fondly. That was the summer he went up north.

By his freshman year in high school, Justin had amassed few friends. But he had Dylan Nelson, and they had the computer club.

Dylan Nelson and his mother, Cynthia, lived close to Justin and his parents, in the worst section of Chester.

Cynthia Nelson was unusual for the neighborhood. She didn't drink or take drugs in a place where most people did. She took care of her house, on a street where no one else did. She attended church on Sunday mornings, in a town where only the oldest unwelded residents still attended.

Chester boasted five church buildings housing three active church populations. One vacant building was long derelict and the other was being taken over by the fire department, which faced no shortage of chemical fires and arson and needed more space.

At thirty-six, Cynthia Nelson was the second-youngest person attending her church.

She liked Chester Congregational. It existed at the liberal end of the Protestant spectrum, where Cynthia was most comfortable. She would have liked an active youth program at her church, but demographics and apathy conspired against her.

There was precisely one youth in regular church attendance, and he shared her last name.

Once again, unlike most of Chester, with their untidy houses and their untidy drug habits, Cynthia Nelson persevered, persuading a bigger church an hour away to drive their minibus all the way to her church to pick up the one or, occasionally, two sad-sack kids who showed up on Sundays.

Dylan Nelson had no choice in the matter of his attendance. His mom brought him each week. The other sad sack was Justin Everly, whose attendance record was less consistent, but who came to hang out with Dylan, and whose parents didn't know or care where he went on Sunday morning, or any other morning.

At Covenant Assembly, Dylan and Justin got to hang out once a week with kids their age in an hour-long discussion group.

Dylan and Justin found it hard to talk in the youth group. They were both shy and painfully aware that there were no designer labels on the clothes they wore, that neither was enrolled in AP calculus, and that no one else in the room gave a shit about anything that mattered to them. In addition to their glaring cultural and social lapses, both boys arrived each Sunday morning in a quasi-catatonic state, brought on by the rigors of their regular Saturday night computer club all-night lock-in, fueled by liters of cola and boxes of cheap pizza.

The other fifteen-year-olds in the youth program were in awe of the seniors who led the program. They were the older brothers and sisters. They were the kicker and the cheerleader and the debate star and the girl who sang the solo at the choir concerts at the high school they all attended.

Dylan and Justin attended another school. One that didn't have a debate team.

When the discussions turned to raising money, Dylan and Justin noticed that glances fell their way. And that was to be expected. Everyone else in the group knew they were from Chester, that they were bussed to Covenant each Sunday.

On a Sunday morning in late spring, the seniors distributed a full-color brochure. One senior had been elected spokesperson, and she spoke eloquently about an annual canoe trip into the deep woods and twisting backwaters of northern Minnesota, sponsored by the church since before the ken of its eldest members. They apportioned space for six adults, six senior staffers, and twenty-four youths on the trip, which consisted of four nights and five days, with a long drive to get there and back, lengthy portages between lakes, lengthy paddles on said lakes, biting insects, accumulated layers of dirt, sunscreen, and insect repellent that required several post-trip showers to dislodge, heavy rain, warm sun, cold nights, curious bears, wet clothes, dull dehydrated meals, primitive latrines, and stubbed toes, all endured while hauling aluminum canoes and cadaver-proportioned canvas backpacks across the wilderness.

Justin and Dylan talked it over on the minibus ride back to Chester. Dylan was honest enough to out himself as a chronic homebody and chose not to head north. He also wasn't sure if his mother could survive the anxiety of her beloved boy being so far away from home.

But in his bedroom, Justin looked at maps and photographs of the area. He learned that the lands close to the border were mostly protected, but that there were copper reserves nearby. The governor had declared the borderlands would not be mined, and a recent poll indicated that the people of the state agreed with the governor.

Justin also learned that, if he traveled there, he would be required to leave no trace. He now knew what a portage was. He kept reading long into the night.

On the following Sunday morning he received good news. The youth minister quietly took him aside. His state of poverty was no secret at the church. There had been several conversations during the week. Did he want to go on the trip? He did. Was money going to be a problem? He admitted that it would be.

The youth minister smiled at him.

Justin was handed a business-size envelope. Inside was a letter stating that a church endowment would cover his camping fees, his spending money, and any additional funds he needed for supplies. A packing list was enclosed, as was an official application form, with the money parts at the bottom of the page carefully inked out.

Justin smiled. He said thank you. He took the contents of the envelope home.

In the weeks that followed, he was supplied with a waterproof duffle bag. This was to house all that he was allowed to bring in the way of personal items. He needed few supplies. His everyday wardrobe was easily raggedy enough to pass serious camping muster. He could swim adequately. He even bought the expensive brand of sandals the packing list recommended.

His authentic facsimile of his father's lethargic scrawl across the bottom of the permission slip was accepted without question.

On the third Sunday after the brochures were handed out, the youth group split into two factions: those going to the waters and those staying behind. Justin and twenty-three other youths were sequestered in a room with the youth leaders and the church adults who were also going. The adults were introduced; they were all parents of kids going on the trip. One was a dentist. His daughter was going.

He told them that there were two possible locations on the lakes to put in. One was at the outfitters. The other was further away, at Selkirk Lake. The dentist had been there before, with his older son, and he preferred Selkirk. The campers and their canoes and their supplies would have to be driven there. It wasn't so convenient. but he thought it was worth it.

Then he told them that the aluminum canoes were old and heavy. But they were inexpensive to rent and indestructible. The outfitters now offered new Kevlar canoes instead. Much lighter. Much easier to carry. But they were more expensive. And they needed to be treated more carefully.

He paused and smiled at his daughter, who smiled back. Another parent spoke up and told everyone that the dentist, Marty, had generously offered to pay the difference between the aluminum and the Kevlar boats.

The rest of the adults and the leaders began to clap and cheer. The youth campers joined in. As the clapping and cheering grew louder, Marty's face grew redder.

They began the drive north long before daylight. Breakfast had been picked up by two parents on their way to the church parking lot; lunch was also on the church, consumed en route at a chain sandwich shop. Later in the afternoon, they stopped at a roadside stand and sampled freshly prepared beef jerky that stained their hands red and instantly downgraded Justin's previous appreciation of the emaciated convenience-store version.

Dylan's mom had driven Justin to the church in the darkness. She had hugged him before she said her goodbyes in the church parking lot.

"I wish Dylan was going with you," she told him.

"Really, Mrs. Nelson?" he had asked her with a grin.

She hesitated. "No, Justin," she finally replied. "Not really."

His own parents were still asleep when he left. He had explained where he was going the night before. They had looked puzzled, but not especially worried or unhappy.

The minivans made good time as they headed north.

When they reached Duluth, the adults found a coffee shop while the youths and their leaders stopped at a funky resale shop where everyone purchased flannel shirts in a series of unflatteringly large sizes, and no one had to shell out more than five dollars.

The next stage of the drive was slower, as highway became one lane, which became bumpy dirt track that rose and fell, stirring up red dust for the last thirty miles, cruelly punishing the suspensions on the late-model vehicles.

At the outfitters, they were oriented in a hurry. They watched a video on leaving no trace, on burying their unused food, on banging two metal pans together loudly when a large bear was visiting their campsite. Their square hulking Duluth packs were already packed with food and tents and cooking supplies and tarps and ropes and sleeping bags and first aid kits and eating utensils. All they had to do was find a corner of the packs to insert their small personal duffels.

After everyone had selected the appropriate sizes of paddles and life jackets, they were escorted out to the canoes. The owner of the outfitters was an Englishman. He had bad teeth, which showed when he smiled and introduced himself. There were yellow canoes that looked new and green canoes that didn't. The owner asked for a volunteer. Several hands went up. He grinned a little nastily and selected the smallest girl.

The owner stood beside a green canoe and explained that the older canoes were to be gradually superseded by the bright new yellow Kevlar models that were every bit as resilient and a good deal lighter. He asked his tiny volunteer if she could pick up the green canoe. She did. He picked one up too. He asked her if she could lift it onto her shoulders. She hesitated. In a fluid motion he flipped his up and over effortlessly. She gamely tried to follow his lead but faltered at the halfway mark. Two parents were quickly at her side, and they spotted her the rest of the way.

The Englishman flipped his canoe back down to the ground. His volunteer was again assisted by the adults.

The owner walked over to the yellow canoes. Once again, he picked it up and flipped it onto his shoulders. He smiled encouragingly at his volunteer. She took a deep breath and tensed. She was slower and less fluid, but she did it. All by herself. She got a huge cheer, to which she responded with a smile.

They both stood poised with the canoes resting and balanced on their respective shoulders. His boat was motionless; hers wobbled back and forth slightly.

"One . . . two . . . THREE!"

They both flipped their canoes back to the ground, simultaneously, and the crowd went wild.

The owner smiled and shook his volunteer's hand before he silently departed.

They carried the featherlight, yellow marvels to the trailers attached to the dust-covered trucks bearing the outfitters logo on the front doors. They loaded the Duluth packs and the paddles and the life jackets into the back of the trucks.

The first day's paddle was an hour and a half across Selkirk Lake, with a stiff and welcome wind behind them, to an assigned campsite, where the group would camp together for the first and only night.

The next day, the adventure would begin in earnest. The first real portage was two hundred rods, followed by a long paddle into wind blowing straight across the aptly if unimaginatively named Big Lake.

They would meet up at the end of the week, to shower luxuriantly at the outfitters, to trade lies, then begin the journey home, pausing once for a last night away from home, suctioning down copious pizzas on a church floor, on one of the hills overlooking the lights of downtown Duluth.

From the start of the trip, Justin was in heaven, and no amount of dirt and diarrhea, bugs and blisters, sunburn and summer storm showers, could bring him back down to earth.

At the close of each day, he sat with his back wedged against a tree. His feet were bare and his sandals were drying in the heat of the late afternoon sun. They always tried to reach a campsite early in the day; dragging the canoes up from the edge of the water and leaving them in plain view was the most effective way to stake a claim. Putting up the tents in daylight was preferable. Later they would make a fire and cook their dinner. Night descended rapidly. In the darkness, the breeze died, and a blanket of insects fell on them.

Justin had bought a map of the waters from the outfitters, which he kept folded inside a sealed plastic bag with a small pack of colored pencils. Most of the campers had brought along paperback books to read. Their phones were all safely locked up in the minivans, since cell service evaporated half an hour away from the outfitters.

Carefully, he retraced the day's route, the portages they had encountered, and the campsite they had chosen. As near as possible, he tried to draw an accurate line across the lakes they had crossed. If he could, he would wander from the sites into the close woods, looking for a walking trail. If he found one, he would draw that on the map too.

By the end of the trip, his map was falling apart. But he was able to pick up several more from the outfitters before he left, and these he worked on at home in the weeks following the trip, painstakingly copying all the information, adding notes to himself on lakes that looked interesting but that had been too remote for his group to reach. His maps began to overflow with too much information, so Justin purchased several cheap notebooks. In these he began to map out future trips.

This was Justin's Everly's finest summer ever.

COLIN

She was standing at Colin's front door forty-three minutes later, smiling. "You do recognize me, then?"

"Yes," was his honest reply.

"Good." Her smile remained.

"I don't remember your name," he was forced to admit.

"That's hardly surprising," she allowed. "It was sixteen years ago."

There was a very long pause.

"And I was different then." Her smile faltered. "You could invite me in."

He did, and she sat down at his kitchen table without being asked. She moved his coffee cup to one side. She glanced out the window. Nothing in her actions gave any indication that she was nervous, or even that she was in a place she had never been before.

He watched her as she made herself completely at home.

This was his house. He was certain that she had never been here before. Colin was aware that he should be concerned.

She wore gym shoes with no socks he could see and khaki shorts that were shorter and tighter than anything Ruby had worn. Her navy-blue T-shirt looked old and comfortable. Her legs and arms were long and dark. Her hair was cut very short, and her eyes were a deep brown behind her glasses. Although, like Colin, she looked close to fifty-five, she gave off an unmistakable vibe that proclaimed her fifty-five to be a much younger fifty-five than his. She was tall, close to his height, and fit, her muscles gathered together in a series of sinewy knots.

He sat down on one of the other three chairs, one he could barely remember having sat on before.

She placed her phone on the kitchen table. Colin noted that hers was the very latest model whereas his was a five-year-old relic that he usually kept inside his pocket.

She looked him in the eye. "I said I was sorry for your loss, and I meant it."

"Thank you. What is it you want with me?"

"I know you have about a year left." It wasn't a question.

"A little more than that." And for a second, he wondered how she could know.

"That's good," she said. "I thought we could date." Her sudden smile was unexpected and a little wild.

He hadn't expected her proposition. "Now?"

"Why not?" Her smile had settled down. She had very white teeth. It was a pleasant smile.

"I'm not sure I'm ready to date."

She pretended to be surprised. "Are you making fun of me?"

"I'm serious."

"You don't have a whole lot of time left to get ready," she observed brightly.

She had a point.

"Maybe I don't want to date anyone. Or maybe I don't want to date you." Did he sound peevish?

"That would be a shame. I thought you used to find me pretty."

"You were pretty." That sounded terrible. "You still are pretty."

"Well, thank you. What else did you think about me?"

"You were the best student I ever had."

"What else?"

"There wasn't anything else."

"Oh yes, there was." She waited for him.

"I felt sorry for you," was what he finally said.

As hard as he tried, Colin couldn't come up with her name. She had registered in one of his summer computer classes. He didn't remember which year. She had been noticeably more attractive than his students generally were. She had been very pretty, and was even more so. She had been younger then. She looked much younger now. She had not looked healthy then. In fact, she had looked seriously ill.

And he had felt sorry for her.

Yet the woman now sitting at his kitchen table was a picture of robust good health.

"You should probably tell me your name," he told her.

"It's Angie," she said. "I had hoped you would remember."

He said he was sorry.

She picked up her phone and wiped at the screen with the loose cotton material of her shirt. "When I took your class, I didn't know anything about computers. I enjoyed the class. Most of your students were determined to be unteachable, and you were patient. I also thought you were adorable."

"Thank you," he said stiffly. "I'm certain I was both."

"I've learned a lot about computers since."

Colin wasn't at all sure where this conversation was going. "Good for you," he said. He was trying to buy time.

"I play a lot of Trench Warfare," she said. "I'm a Field

Marshall."

"How much did you have to spend to get to that level?"

She shook her head and smiled at him. "I've spent nothing."

Colin couldn't help but be impressed. "Well done," he said.

"You and your son created the game."

"I helped a little."

"It's a wonderful game."

There was a pause. It was apparently Colin's turn to speak. "I'm older than you."

She nodded. "Twenty years."

"You could date someone younger."

"I have," she giggled more than she laughed. "I'm unattached right now. This is your big chance. You should take it. You don't have long."

He snorted out a response. "Thank you so much for reminding me."

She smiled encouragingly. "I didn't mean it that way. It's just that I don't like to stay unattached for long."

The clock was running. "I see," he said at last.

Angie continued, "When I was in your class, I promised myself that I would come for you. When you were free. If I was free at the same time. And here I am. We're both free. I knew that your wife was a little older, so I knew she would conclude before you. I don't have anyone now. Do I sound a little creepy?"

The answer was more than a little, but he chose not to admit it. Instead he said, "I might not want to date. I mean I might not want to date anyone."

"I know," she said. "You might not. In fact, you probably

don't. You probably want to grieve. I understand. But you can grieve and date at the same time. That would be fine with me. Anyway, I wanted to ask, Was your wife nice? You don't need to answer. I imagine she was."

"How did you know my wife was dead? And how did you know she was older?"

She waited a long time before she answered. "I could lie to you."

"How could you lie?"

"I could say I read her obituary in the paper."

"But you didn't."

"No, I didn't, she said. "I accessed your records. Both of your records. After I had been in your class I made a note to myself. When you would be free. When she would . . ." Angie didn't finish the sentence.

Colin was incredulous. "So, you waited for her to die?"

"Not exactly. I didn't wait. I just made a note to myself. I really do sound creepy, don't I?"

When he spoke again his voice was softer. "I always thought so."

She looked confused. "What did you think?"

"You asked me about my wife," he was almost whispering. "I did think she was nice."

There was a long silence after that, which she eventually broke. "I should tell you that I don't need much."

He must have looked confused. "Much what?"

"Much money. Fancy things. Stuff. I have more than enough."

"What do you do Angie? How do you live?"

"I mostly steal."

"You look very healthy," he observed. "I remember you

weren't always."

"You really do remember me. I wasn't sure if you would. I'm flattered. But you're right. I was getting sick then. Now I'm much better."

"How did you get better?"

"I told you," she said. "I steal."

He considered this for a moment, then he spoke. "I could make some coffee."

It was her turn to do some considering. "Do you like to drink coffee?"

"I do. Although I don't usually drink more than one cup in the morning."

"Have you had one cup this morning?"

"I have."

"It's no longer morning. Do you drink coffee in the afternoon?"

He spoke guardedly. "Sometimes."

"Then we could have afternoon coffee," she reasoned.

He stood up decisively. "I'll make more."

"I'd like that," she said. "It's going to be nice that we both like to drink coffee."

"It may not be enough to sustain a relationship," he observed, before changing the subject. "I need to know something about you."

She was grinning. "Of course," she said." What do you want to know?"

"There are two things."

She pretended to sigh. "What two things?"

"You're not sick anymore."

She nodded. "What else?"

"And you steal."

She was still nodding. "What would you like to know about me first?"

After Colin made the afternoon coffee, he learned more than two things about Angie.

The first thing he learned was her last name.

Angie Rennie could track her family back through four generations, to a plantation in South Carolina. She could also trace her Parkinson's disease for the same time span. In the years after she attended Colin's class, the disease worsened: her hands shook and her balance faltered, it was harder for her to talk and to be understood when she did, her muscles tightened, and her back began to curve. She took medications, she exercised daily in water, and when she concentrated, she was able to subvert some of the symptoms for a while, but the effort was exhausting.

She had been thirty-eight when she attended Colin's computer class. In seventeen years, she would be officially scanned, and she would fail. Her next years would come with increasing pain and accelerating decay. There was a very good chance she would die young. There was a lesser chance she wouldn't, but neither prospect was especially attractive.

Angie sipped her coffee.

"I paid close attention to everything you told us in that class."

"I remember that you stared at me a lot."

"That was only because you were cute."

"That would certainly explain it."

Over the next four years, Angie Rennie hacked her way into all kinds of computer systems: the military, big banks, hospitals, government agencies.

Colin wondered, "Was it difficult?"

"Hardly. Hacking in is easy. Not leaving a trail is the hard part. I accessed offshore banks and transferred small amounts from certain accounts. I picked my victims carefully. Mostly white-collar types. People who were not very interested in having their tax shelters and insider-traded profits made public. So, they were willing to take the small losses. I always made sure to leave them with plenty."

Angie Rennie stopped talking. Colin watched her. He said nothing. He waited.

Finally, she spoke quietly. "But my health began to get worse."

Colin interrupted her. "You look fine now."

"I am fine now. I was welded nine years ago."

He took a deep breath. "How the hell is that possible? And even if it was possible, what difference would it make?"

As best she could, she told him.

Angie had broken into government records, altered her age, and taken the scan when she was forty-four, although she had been advised against the last part. Visibly sick people were discouraged from wasting time on a test that would only confirm what everybody already knew. If they were seriously, irrevocably ill, they would fail the scan, and the weld, even if they could somehow have it, would be worthless. Angie had anticipated a scene, an argument, but she also knew that the hospital authorities would ultimately acquiesce. The scan was an inalienable right that everyone possessed, no matter what condition he or she was in. The authorities also knew that there was no way to cheat the scan; you would either pass or you would fail.

And Angie Rennie would fail. She would not be welded.

"So, how were you able to pass the scan?"

Angie shook her head, then she shrugged. "I didn't. I failed miserably."

"So how—?

She cut him off. "All I had to do was hack into the government records and change my scan result from a fail to a pass."

He had to laugh. "So, you cheated on the final."

"Yup," she agreed cheerfully. "Twice, in fact. I cheated once to take the final, and, after I took it, I changed that nasty F to an A."

"And then, they welded you?"

She nodded slowly and smiled mysteriously. "I worried about the scan itself. I was really ill. I looked really ill. I shook. I thought they'd find a way to not scan me. So, I had a few drinks and poured a few more all over myself. I told them I was a drunk and I had the shakes and I felt terrible. I'm not sure if I was believable. But they scanned me. When I went for the weld, they checked my scan report more than once. But I had already changed the result. According to the records, I passed the scan. So, they welded me."

"They welded you?"

She nodded slowly. "Once again, I must have looked terrible. I told them I was still drinking. I smelled terrible, and I shook. At least I was consistent. And I had passed the scan."

"What was the point? You were really sick. The weld only works on healthy people."

"What did I have to lose?"

The weld and the scan were often referred to as miracles. But they were rigidly controlled and narrowly defined miracles. The scan would only pass those on whom the weld could work. The weld would sustain health. It would prolong health. But it was not able to heal.

But there were sick people with desperate hopes and there were fears and there were rumors. And there were freakish occurrences. The weld would very occasionally fail. A clean scan would still precede a premature death from what should have been a red flag, a genetically observable warning sign.

And sometimes a sick body would inexplicably rally. A scan would fail and, years or months later, an inherited illness would recess. An equilibrium of health would be restored, without the benefit of government-sanctioned genetic tampering.

There were other rumors, too, of clandestine black-market welds performed on the sick. Mostly these measures failed. But there were claims of mysterious cures, of lives transformed, made both longer and better.

"What happened to your Parkinson's?"

Angie offered a smirk of mocking innocence. "Do I look like I have Parkinson's now?"

"And there are no symptoms left?"

"None." She was still smirking.

"How long will you live?"

Angie Rennie pretended to look befuddled. "Now, how would I know that?" she said. "I'm assuming I'll get the All Clear Twenty. Just like you. Just like the regular weldees. But I really don't know for sure. How could I? Maybe I'll live another ten years. Maybe I'll live to seventy-five. Maybe I'll live forever."

"How did you get into the government computer system?"

"It wasn't hard to get in. It was very hard to get out. It was almost impossible to get out and leave no trace." She looked at him craftily. "But you did teach me well."

"You're quite obviously kidding. Because that's a whole lot more than I could ever do. Have you been back inside the government system since then?" he asked her.

Angie looked serious. "Never. I'd be too scared. It was difficult. I got lucky. If I try to go in again it might trigger something and then they'll notice me." She shook her head firmly. "I don't want that to happen. I don't want to get noticed. I want to go on living. And I want to go on living well."

They drank their coffees in a companionable silence.

After a while she spoke. "I like your garden."

He was going to tell her that Ruby was the gardener, but he stopped. Instead he asked an unrelated question. "Where do you live?"

She looked coy. "Very close."

"Do you like to walk?" he asked.

"I prefer to run."

"We could go for a walk. Or I could go for a walk. You could run."

She seemed pleased at his proposal. "We could. It could be like a date."

"Perhaps."

"When do you want to go?"

He surprised himself with his answer: "We could go now."

"Now?" she said smiling. He had surprised her too.

"Now," he said more firmly. "As you said, I don't have much time."

The forest preserve was north and west of where Colin lived. He would take her there, where she would doubtless run fast and lap him.

A city bus route ran near the preserve, but Colin decided that he would drive Angie there. Ruby always thought that Colin drove too fast. His car had a six-cylinder 3.6 liter engine, with all-wheel drive and 280 horsepower that could get to sixty without too much fuss in well under six seconds.

There were newer and faster machines. But he was happy with his.

Colin watched Angie as she got in and adjusted her seatbelt. He was certain she would not complain if he drove fast.

So, he did.

While he walked and she ran and they had their first date, he would consider three conundrums: the significance of the number two-three-eight-one; the mystery of Angie Rennie's disappearing disease; and Elliot Devine and his remarkable resurrection.

∞

At the forest preserve, Angie Rennie walked beside Colin. Or at least she tried to walk beside Colin.

"Do you always walk this fast?" She was breathless.

He laughed sheepishly. "I was trying to walk slower for you."

"I don't even run this fast."

"I'm sorry."

"Don't be." She began to mumble to herself, "I'll just have to go faster. This isn't right. You're supposed to be the old guy here. This is just wrong."

They were on the preserve path. Angie pointed to his side. "What have you got in the bag?"

He pretended to be defensive. "Stuff."

She pushed harder. "What kind of stuff?"

"Bottles of water. Granola bars. Apples. That kind of stuff."

"For yourself?"

"Of course not. For both of us."

She looked both delighted and incredulous. "You packed these before we left?"

He suddenly felt foolish. "You used the bathroom," he said. "And what if I did?"

She marveled, "Without me even asking. Did your wife know she was spoiled?"

"I don't think she saw it that way."

Later they stopped at a picnic area. He had also packed four paper towels that he had folded neatly and diagonally. She wiped stray pieces of apple from her mouth with the one he handed her. She looked as if she wanted to say something.

But she didn't. And then she did.

"So, there's no trace of your Mr. Devine?"

Colin shook his head as he finished his water and threw the empty bottle into the recycling bin inside the corrugated metal enclosure. They sat together on benches at a large wooden table.

He had told her about the brief obituary and the much more lavish financial postscripts he had also found online.

Elliot Devine had been wealthy when he concluded, and the planned disposition of his considerable estate had initially been a simple affair. All funds were to be bequeathed to the Natural Boundary Foundation, an organization with a post office box in Duluth, Minnesota, and a website filled with impressive pictures of forests and lakes.

But how often noble intentions can go astray.

In one of the tabloid publications, they were referred to gleefully as the divine Devine women. Neither of his ex-wives had anything nice to say about him in print. Each had borne him two daughters, and all four teenage girls, like their two mothers, were sharply etched blondes with laser-like blue eyes fixed firmly on the prize. All six had lawyered up even before Devine's conclusion. All six were reported to be much happier sans his physical presence in their lives, but all six were more than willing to countenance his monetary presence, in the form of financial settlements.

The tree huggers in Duluth would surely have to wait.

"And you're sure it was him you saw at the airport?"

"I'm sure," he said.

Angie had her phone in her hands. As she typed furiously, she asked, "When did he die?"

Colin told her.

Then she asked. "When did he try to buy your son's company?"

He told her that, too.

"Don't you think that's odd?"

He had had the same thought.

She put it into words. "Why would you want to spend your money if you were going to die so soon? Didn't he want the foundation in Duluth to have it all?"

"He did. But maybe he thought a long-term portfolio item was a good thing for the nature folks in Minnesota to have."

Angie was talking to herself. "So, he was trying to invest. A leveraged hostile buy. In Trench Warfare. Maybe." She still didn't sound convinced. "But I think a nonprofit would probably be happier with a cash gift."

"Maybe he wanted to keep some of it away from the Devine women."

"Perhaps." She continued, "Were they after his stuff even before he died?"

"Apparently."

"How has that battle ended?"

"It isn't close to ending. They're all fighting it out in court."

"Not quite all. Elliot Devine isn't," Angie observed. Then she looked thoughtful. "There's another reason Devine might have been trying to keep investing right before he died."

Colin smiled at her. "I think I know where you're heading."

She continued anyway. "Because he wasn't planning on actually dying."

"But if he's going to live, he's got no money. The Natural Boundary Foundation was supposed to receive his whole estate."

Angie laughed. "You mean the whole Elliot Devine estate. If he's alive, he's no longer going around using the same name. You said his appearance was changed."

"Some," Colin said. "But not enough. Maybe he didn't die. Maybe he didn't conclude."

Angie stopped typing. "I've just checked the same government records you did. He clearly did."

Moments later Angie showed her phone screen to Colin. It showed a man emerging from the snugness of a small tent. He was unkempt, and he was smiling. A cluster of evergreen trees surrounded the tent, the charred remains of a campfire nearby.

Colin slowly nodded. He was looking at Elliot Devine in his natural habitat.

Angie continued to scroll rapidly through a collection of tiny images.

"He certainly did like the great outdoors," she remarked.

"I'm sure he still does. What are you finding?"

Angie shook her head sadly. "The recent stuff about him is all legal stuff. The fight in court over his estate. Before that, there were obituaries, and before that, lots of technology buyouts and hostile takeovers; all the business he was involved in before his conclusion. As I said, there are lots of photos of him either getting into or out of a canoe or in and out of a tent."

"There's nothing to suggest he's still alive?

"Nothing."

"What are you finding that I couldn't?"

"Not much." She was still typing. "His companies are liquidated. His investments aren't active."

"He's dead," Colin reminded her, unnecessarily.

"Elliot Devine's certainly dead. But I have a theory: He went after TW and your son because he wanted something for his next life. It would have been his first investment."

"He was still Devine when he tried to buy from Tony."

"He could have transferred ownership before he concluded."

Colin considered this carefully.

"Did I mention there is an Elliot Devine still living?" Angie said suddenly.

"Really?"

"Really. He's in his early twenties. He's a professional soccer player. He lives in Scotland. He's very good, apparently."

Colin concluded, "I think we can safely assume he's not our man."

Angie nodded. She continued to type furiously.

"Devine has a homepage."

"Is it still active?"

She shook her head. "It's still up. There's been no new content posted since his death. A lot of his outdoor photos are taken from the same geographic area."

"Where?" Colin asked.

She answered, "The Frontier Waters. In northern Minnesota. North of Duluth. Very close to the border. The whole area is national forest."

Colin was smiling at her. "Have you ever been there?" he asked.

Angie shook her head.

"We have a lake house up north. It's very near there. *I* have a lake house," he amended.

She said nothing.

"I think Elliot Devine is still alive."

The typing paused. "If you're right, we have ourselves a fake conclusion."

"Is there such a thing?"

"I don't see why not. The next question is, why is he still alive?"

"I don't know," Colin answered. "Maybe someone made a mistake."

"Or maybe someone didn't."

"And then we have the illegal weld that magically cured your illness."

"It would seem so."

"Are welds supposed to do that?"

"Not that I'm aware of. My understanding is that they prevent any illnesses occurring. If you already have an illness you don't get to have a weld. And even if you did it wouldn't do any good."

"Maybe you're some kind of freak."

She replied curtly, "Why, thank you."

"You know what I mean."

"I do. I suppose I could be. Or maybe I just got better all by myself."

"It's been known to happen."

"It has."

"But I don't believe you just got better."

"Nope," Angie said, looking up from her phone. "Me neither. But you know something? We don't know that much about welds. And when I say we, I don't just mean you and me. Even science doesn't know much more. About how they work." She paused. "Supposing you have an illness and you get scanned and you fail and years later your illness goes away. Can you get scanned again? And will you pass? And if you do, can you get a weld, then? And if you can get a weld, does it still last for twenty years? Or only until you reach seventy-five? What happens in these cases? Because you know that has to occur sometimes."

"I agree. My understanding is that the scan identifies and predicts illnesses."

"Mine too. And I understand that part. But sometimes people must just get better."

"Maybe not that often."

"No," she had to agree. "Maybe not often." She paused for dramatic effect. "But sometimes."

"What was your other point?" he asked her.

"Do you know why people get scanned at fifty-five?"

He thought about it. "I don't," he admitted. "I know that governments all got together and decided on fifty-five. But I don't know why."

She shrugged. "I don't know either."

They lapsed into perplexed silence at that point in the conversation.

The silence ended as Angie began to type again. "I've found more records."

"Public records?"

"Well, almost public records. The newspapers don't specify the exact amount of money Devine is leaving to the foundation in Duluth. But I found it somewhere else. No wonder the Devine women aren't letting go. It's an awful lot of money." She paused.

"How much—"

"—Is an awful lot of money? I'm glad you asked. I believe the answer would be three billion dollars."

In the middle distance they could both hear the low hum of commuter traffic.

∞

The forest preserve housed a four-mile circuit of asphalt path that bikes, dogs, and walkers shared uneasily. What was intended to be unattended grass, which would by design revert back into Midwest prairie, was instead being subjected to much greater rainfalls and much denser urbanization and attendant runoff. It would be swamp within two decades. The preserve transitioned organically into a neighborhood of larger four-bedroom homes. For the most part they were endearingly scruffy, beset by tangles of surrounding garden, which, at this time of year, were lush and moss-steeped, punctuated by patches of stagnant lawn that, like the preserve, seldom completely drained, acting as so many mosquito incubators in the summer months.

"Is there a granola bar in there for me?" Angie asked.

Without a word, Colin opened the bag and handed her one.

"I've already used my paper towel." Angie made a sad face at him.

In silence, he handed her another, which Angie used to swipe quickly at the side of his face. He looked at her curiously.

She grinned at him. "There was still some apple there."

"No, there wasn't."

"It seemed like a motherly thing to do."

"You're not my mother."

"True."

They drove home later in the afternoon. It transpired, as she had already told him, that she did live nearby. Less than two miles away. When he parked the car outside her house, she thanked him for the ride.

"You walked to my house today." It was not a question.

She shook her head. "I considered it. But I was lazy. So, I took the train."

"How did you know I would be home?"

"Aren't you supposed to be in mourning?"

While she had a point, he was not convinced that some technological manner of surveillance was not also involved.

She waited for him to ask. He didn't. So, she had to ask him, "Can I see you again soon?"

"How soon?" he asked her.

She replied, "Very soon."

"Another date?"

"That's the plan."

"I'm going for a walk tomorrow," he said carefully.

"The same place?"

Colin shook his head. "I was thinking of heading to the beach for my lunch."

"It'll be more crowded."

He shook his head again. "I go north, to the edge of the city. And the weather forecast isn't that good."

"Will you be bringing the snacks again?"

He shrugged to indicate helplessness. "It's what I do."

Angie giggled, leaned in, and kissed him on the cheek. Then she got out of the car and ran to her front door. "Text me tomorrow when you're ready to go," she shouted. "You can pick me up."

He shouted back, "I don't know your number."

"There's a text on your phone. It's from me," she yelled at him. "You just have to reply."

The front door of her tiny bungalow was open, and then she disappeared.

Colin sat in his car for a moment with the engine running. There was a possibility that Angie Rennie was not his type.

Her front yard was dry mud and seriously neglected.

Her front door all but begged for a painting.

He should be grieving in earnest.

She was young. He had a little more than a year to live.

In his heart of hearts, he could not dispel the thought that she was only dating him for the snacks.

Which was probably just as well, because it crossed Colin's mind that Angie Rennie might be better off as his research sidekick than a romantic companion.

He needed a sidekick. He had several mysteries to solve.

Before he drove away, he looked at his phone. There was indeed a text, short and to the point: *Thanx for the snax.*

And there it was. Proof positive that the way to her heart was by way of her stomach.

Yet, Colin Tugdale couldn't wait for tomorrow.

∞

What on earth would Ruby think?

This was the question Colin pondered in the early hours of the evening, as he sat with a glass of red wine, on a metal chair, at a metal table, on the small concrete patio behind his house. There were eight-foot-high redwood-stained fences draped in purple-blue clematis on two sides. The third side stood open, overlooking a patch of well-trimmed grass.

The Tugdales' house in the city was a trim three-bedroom, one-level affair. By contrast, his neighbor's was a three-flat behemoth standing in the center of a double lot. The top floor boasted a flimsy deck construction that buttressed the back of the building, with a well-used barbeque unit that was brutally overworked during the late summer months of night-time baseball.

There was no shortage of grilling and yelling tonight. They were unceasingly loud and boisterous people. Colin liked them well enough most of the time, that is, until he tried to go to bed early. When there was a doubleheader on the television they often transported out onto the deck. Doubleheaders usually necessitated an extended round of screaming and the enthusiastic tapping of a second keg.

Well, honey, you did tell me to try something new.

He wasn't certain that dating this quickly was what she had in mind. Perhaps she imagined him taking up needlepoint or birdwatching. But, as hard as he tried to make himself feel guilty, he found that he couldn't. Ruby would want him to be happy. She would want him not to grieve. She would want him not to waste away. She wouldn't want him to linger after her and then die without consequence, a pointlessly squandered year or so after her.

When one partner was scheduled for conclusion, it was not unheard of for the other to choose death at that same moment. Some of these attendant deaths came with sound rationales; a concluding spouse may have a non-welded partner with health issues, for whom the future might seem too frightening and uncertain. For that spouse, a companionable exit might be deemed the wiser course. And there were couples simply unable to imagine a life apart.

Colin's and Ruby's times of conclusion were relatively close. And for this reason, they had discussed the question of Colin pre-concluding with Ruby.

It had been a short discussion. Colin had tenderly raised the possibility, and Ruby had bluntly shot the concept down in three short words. They had quickly moved on to other topics of conversation.

For the record, the words in question were: *Don't be stupid.*

Colin sagely reasoned that he could not be blamed if he chose to spend his final year in a wallow of wanton womanizing.

But it would hardly be that. He would make the most of his short time. He would not feel guilty, for any number of reasons, including his sneaking suspicion that Ruby Tugdale would have found Angie Rennie at the very least, curious. *I only have one year left.* He suspected he would remind himself of this often.

When he turned his laptop on, he was not surprised to discover that he had several emails from the curious Ms. Rennie.

She had forwarded him a copy of the Devine beneficence document. Colin sipped his wine as a bright red cardinal, the gaudy male of the species, landed on the bird feeder attached to the wall of the garage at the bottom of the yard. Colin smiled to himself. He had recently remembered to load the feeder, and the bird made a welcome change from the usual battalions of fat, pampered, and singularly unwelcome squirrels.

Angie had also unearthed some general information on the Natural Boundary Foundation. There wasn't much. The NBF was not a public but a private foundation. As a result, they had no board of freely elected well-wishers, and fewer of the usual philanthropic requirements for financial or ideological transparency. They had a board of directors and a chairman, all elected by donors. They were seemingly not required to list either their donors or their elected officials. Their donations were used to further their objectives. Their assets were not listed. Nor were their objectives stated.

Angie had been unable to find listings of their founder, their chairman, their current or past board members, or much of anything else.

Like the pictures on Elliot Devine's home page, the images on the NBF site were from the Frontier Waters.

Angie's next email contained nothing Colin didn't already know.

The Frontier began two hours northeast of Duluth, Minnesota, and stretched up to the Canadian border. This was land that, dating from times past, had been extensive swaths of state and national forest, riddled with no-wake lakes, bleak and cold and inaccessible in winter, accessible in summer along dirt roads and hiking trails, but penetrated the more deeply with canoes, to be paddled, and painstakingly portaged.

The NBF website accepted credit card donations online and directed checks to the address of a post office box in Duluth.

The foundation did not specify whether or not donations were tax-deductible.

The website was a masterpiece of evasiveness, with no discussion of what the NBF did, or what they wanted to do. They seemed to be hazily pro-nature and vaguely and indefinably anti pretty much everything else. At the least, they stood opposed to all forms of government intervention.

Colin looked at a few more pictures of lakes and trees before closing his laptop and finishing his wine. It was still early. The deck next door was at full capacity, and the timbers were heaving under the strain. The home team was winning comfortably.

He went inside.

It would be another hour before the visitors staged a late rally.

For the weld widower Colin Tugdale, that next portion of the night stretched out noisily, and sleeplessly.

But it ended with a narrow victory for the hometown heroes, and several hours of belated shut-eye for Colin.

∞

Angie was talking to her phone. "That's weird."

Colin was talking to the wet road through the car windshield. "What's weird?"

They were northbound on the main road running along

the coastline of the city. The sky was cloudy, and a feather-light drizzle was tormenting the sensors on the windshield wipers.

Colin waited for an answer that was not immediately forthcoming.

"I have a windbreaker in the trunk that will fit you," Colin told her a moment later.

She smiled. "Of course you do."

Angie was wearing the same shorts as yesterday, and a dark green T-shirt. She was cold, if the proliferation of goosebumps on her bare brown arms was any indication.

"We could close the windows," he offered.

"No. Don't. I'm okay being cold."

Colin tried again. "So, what's so weird?"

"Just so you know, I'm not a paranoid person."

"I'm glad to hear it."

She put her phone down and turned to face him. "I get a text alert if someone runs a credit check on me. It doesn't happen often; maybe twice in the past five years. I own my house. I don't own a car. I've had my credit cards forever, and I don't use them much. My alert doesn't tell me who requested the credit check, but it tells me which company ran the check, which isn't that helpful, since there are only about a half dozen credit outfits. They're the ones you see on TV ads offering you a free report if you sign up for extra protection you don't need. I can speak from experience when I say that running a check on someone is pretty easy."

He didn't need to ask, but he blurted it out just the same: "You ran a credit check on me, didn't you?"

"You might be a gold digger."

"That's true," he allowed. "Although you appear to be the one chasing me."

"So, some credit company I've never heard of just ran a credit check on me."

"That's weird."

"That's what I said."

"Are you buying a house?"

Angie ignored him. He tried again.

"A car?"

"I run my own credit checks."

"How does that work?"

"Do you really want to know?"

"Is there a simple version of the answer?"

"No, there isn't."

"You checked on me." Did he sound offended?

"I did. You're a loan shark's worst nightmare. Have you ever bought anything on credit?"

He grew defensive. "Our house. We had a mortgage once."

She was dismissive. "It's been paid off for years. You paid your mortgage off ahead of schedule, which most financial planners would tell you is foolish. I also ran a second check."

"On?"

"The Natural Boundary Foundation. But I failed. The system kicked me out. I learned nothing. And I think I triggered their response. Which was to run a check of their own."

"Can you tell if they were more successful?"

She smiled without warmth. "I can't tell for sure. But I can make a guess."

"And?"

"I'm assuming they found out more about me than I found out about them."

∞

Colin took the last exit toward the lake, before the coast road turned sharply into the first of the suburbs north of the city.

It was unseasonably chilly, and, with the exception of a few mouthy seagulls, Colin and Angie had the beach to themselves.

Colin twisted open a small flask of coffee. He sat down on a wooden bench and looked out across the water before he poured half the contents of the flask into the plastic cup, electing to drink his share straight from the container. Angie was wearing the windbreaker he had offered her. Moments later, she pulled her shoes off and ran toward the waves. Her movement momentarily scattered the birds, who quickly and expectantly regrouped at the sight of the sandwiches Colin was pulling from his lunch bag.

The waves were higher than the lack of wind would indicate, and Angie let out a wild laugh as the bottom inch of her shorts was instantly soaked. She shouted at him as she ran back across the wet sand, "The water's warm!"

Colin said nothing. As she got closer she saw that tears were running down his face. She held him gently at first, but as he sobbed, he collapsed more fully into her arms and her grip grew tighter.

Colin was wretchedly aware of her body. The closeness of it. How strongly she held him. His own arms circled her waist and he pulled her closer. He wanted to kiss her almost as much as he wanted to be held and to keep on crying.

The conflicting emotions were wonderful.

"I miss her," he finally whispered into her ear. He pulled away and tried to point to the tidemark on Angie's shorts. As he did, he forced himself to smile. "She would have done the very same thing."

She grinned. "I did say you can grieve and date."

They shared sandwiches with the less-than-patient birds, and both their feathered friends and the courting/mourning couple ate in silence.

He drove Angie home from the beach later in the afternoon. The rain had grown stronger, and the temperature had dropped. No one else joined them by the waterfront, and even the gulls had abandoned them after confirming that all the edibles in Colin's bag were gone.

Colin felt foolish. He had cried for a long time, and this was clearly not the ideal way to comport oneself on a second date. Of course, he had not been on a second date, or any other kind of date, for a long time, but he was still fairly certain that extended blubbering was not the recommended route.

However, in many ways he felt better. It was clear that he had needed a good cry, and he had certainly enjoyed holding Angie.

He looked over at Angie as he pulled up at her house. "I'm sorry."

She smiled as she typed. "Don't be. Text me when you want to go out again."

"When should I do that?"

"Soon." She didn't stop texting. She was still smiling. "Text me very soon."

He waited until she was inside before he drove away.

Later that evening, Colin again flaunted his cavalier new attitude toward money.

He had noted several places on the Natural Boundary Foundation website where donations could be made. He positioned his cursor over the first one he found. As he pulled his credit card from his wallet, he considered the amount he would give. A dollar would be too small. A million would be too large. There was certainly a lot of room in between. He was curious to see what, if any, response he would receive. This was lost money. There was no tax deduction to be had. If the NBF was legitimate, he was giving his money to a place that may well deserve it. If it wasn't . . .

Angie might have stirred the pot with her credit check, whereas a donation seemed less provocative. And perhaps the response would tell him something about the foundation that he didn't already know.

Five boxes, marked 10 dollars, 100 dollars, 1,000 dollars, 10,000 dollars, and other. Colin went straight for the middle box and clicked.

He hadn't needed his credit card, as his laptop stored a copy of all the relevant information. The transaction was over in seconds. In an instant, he received an automated thank you. He would be interested to see if a more personal reply followed.

Next, Colin called the airline he had flown home on and spoke to a customer service representative. He told her how much he had enjoyed flying first class and she thanked him. He asked if it would be possible to enroll in the rewards program permanently. He was once again thanked. After that there was a pause in the conversation. Before he was put on hold, Colin could hear a computer keyboard begin to pitter-patter in the background.

His creditworthiness was doubtlessly being assessed. He thought briefly of Angie's unexpected inquiry.

Colin Tugdale had a lot of money. But did he have enough money?

As he waited, it occurred to him that the brevity of his remaining lifespan would work in his favor here. He could easily afford to fly first class because, after all, he was only going to be flying first class for a year or so. And after that, he wasn't going to be flying anywhere. As if to confirm this, the representative was back, and she had some good news for Colin.

He would get his rewards card in the next few days, and he was given a temporary four-digit access code.

The numbers were an unremarkable six-two-six-one, which he dutifully wrote down.

He was asked if he wanted to book a flight tonight. He declined. When he asked her what his rewards status would cost, he was quoted a figure considerably higher than he had imagined. He hesitated for a moment. But only for a moment.

He even remembered to thank her as he hung up.

Colin was absurdly pleased with himself. His next year of flying would be in the lap of luxury. He had just spent a great deal of money, and he didn't care. Tomorrow, he would be driving out to the airport for some overpriced pampering and amateur sleuthing.

Ruby had told him to try something new. He felt that, in many ways, he very definitely was.

He would need to get his rest first.

No ballgame that night, and the gods of sleep and/or baseball smiled down.

∞

Colin Tugdale was dreaming. He knew it, even as he dreamed.

The three rooms in the large house lay far apart. The house itself was an old manor house. He was somewhere in England. Or, at least, he was somewhere in a stylized Masterpiece Theatre *version of England. The house stood austere and Georgian on a hill, high above a significant acreage of land. Yet the land wasn't all attendant to the manor. There was working farmland. There was also a neglected greenhouse, with cracked and broken windows that threatened the existence of the non-native plants huddled inside. He was aware that there were pretty, moss-draped, thatch-roofed cottages further away, with well-tended squares of garden allotments, and there were nameless peasants who tended the allotments, or were in service up at the manor, or who free held in the wheat fields that Colin instinctively knew were a portion of the manor lands.*

Had the concept of freeholding ever factored into one of his dreams before? Colin thought not.

And yet he, Colin Tugdale, a commoner of little import, was attending a party in the manor house. He wore, implausibly, a tweed jacket. He also sported a white shirt and a red plaid tie. He held a full glass in his hand. He hadn't drunk any of it, although he thought it might be sherry. He was surrounded by people, men and women to whom he was pointedly not talking. Men and women, it should be said, who were equally pointedly not talking to him.

Colin was in the first of three rooms.

The manor house presumably had many other rooms, but they were irrelevant to his dream's narrative. The three rooms were high-ceilinged, with plaster walls crumbling elegantly, hung with oil paintings depicting stiff-backed earls a-hunting on horseback and beagles a-beagling in ritualized hunt scenes. Somewhere at the periphery of the stylized motif lurked the requisite lowly fox, no doubt a-paralyzed with fear.

In the second room, his dead wife Ruby stood surrounded by other women. She was replete with a collection of blood-red jewels and an elegant powder blue floor-length dress, an ensemble she would never have countenanced in real life. All the women in the room were clad in similar garb.

In the third room stood Angie Rennie. She struck quite the figure, in cream-colored jodhpurs, knee-high black leather riding boots spit-polished to a high sheen, and a tight black jacket with a crisp white cotton blouse underneath. She held a crop and hat in one hand and a fluted champagne glass in the other. Colin wasn't sure if the real Angie would ever be seen in this ensemble, but he found it easier to imagine her in hunting duds than Ruby in her getup, or him in his, for that matter.

Like Ruby, Angie was surrounded by other women, in this case, all in riding attire.

In the second and third rooms, all the women were dressed similarly. In both rooms, there was a large crowd. In both rooms, there were no men in attendance.

Colin's dream, like a great many dreams, was a study in motionlessness.

Although Colin Tugdale would spend the length of his dream desiring to get to one or other of the other rooms, he was utterly unsuccessful. He was never able to leave the room he was in. He pushed his way through gathered groups, he mumbled his apologies, he elbowed largely oblivious guests out of his way, but his ultimate destination was a faraway door that he never managed to reach.

Despite the enduring frustration he felt, he was also, within the logic of the dream, slightly thankful. Because it was never clear to him which of the two rooms he would or should head for, if he was ever to manage to engineer his escape. And his indecision left him feeling a mixture of guilt and guilty relief.

Colin was perpetually uncomfortable in his dream. For one thing, he was too warm in his wool jacket. The party was a daytime affair, and the sun was high and bright in the sky outside the house. He could see a circular drive at the front of the house, composed of tiny pale red stones that crunched satisfyingly under the weight of luxury car tires. There was a pond with a statue in the center of the drive. The statue, made of green-mossed stone, depicted a partially clothed nymph brandishing a chalice in her weed-draped hands.

Colin wasn't entirely sure what a nymph was; his sense of nymphs and sprites and fairies in general was distressingly vague. But in his dream the statue was unquestionably a nymph.

In his dream Colin was aware of several other facts. Ruby and Angie knew each other. Ruby and Angie liked each other. Ruby and Angie were both anxious to see Colin. Ruby and Angie also could not leave their respective rooms. Ruby and Angie were not aware that this was a dream. Colin, on the other hand, was.

As the futility of his situation showed no likelihood of ending, Colin had no choice but to force his dream to end.

But Colin Tugdale still awoke from his dream with the pervasive sense that he was guilty of something.

JUSTIN

There was no longer a paper for Justin to deliver. He was not due to work at the diner until Monday. The party for Avril on Sunday would be an excruciating experience he was better off not enduring. He felt bad about blowing off the Tap in the evening. It would be a busy night. Andy had been a good boss, even if Andy's father had taken Justin's college money from his worthless parents. On Monday morning, the Tidy and Ruiz families would manage just fine without him.

Justin rode the local bus for two hours, heading north and west to the city in the early morning.

Although it picked up few people, the bus made slow progress. At one point, the driver pulled up outside a coffee shop to use the restroom. Justin told the driver he would get himself something at the shop. The driver offered no objection, and Justin bought a large coffee.

He had packed his duffel the night before. It was the same one he had taken north a decade before. Packing was easy, because he had considered and reconsidered the selection of contents at least a million times.

He had made many modifications. The things he had taken the first time had been adequate at best. Now he included a small towel that would become a blanket or a pillow, dry fast, and pack easily. Swimsuit. T-shirts. A waterproof jacket. His water shoes he would wear. He intended to walk more and paddle less, and sandals wouldn't be substantial enough to hike very far. He had observed one adult on the first trip pull on a pair of thick wool socks at the end of each day. It was, the adult proudly remarked, his single item of shameless luxury.

Justin had looked on enviously. Now he had his very own pair.

He had notebooks and pencils and a map of the canoe area wilderness that a kind teacher at the junior college had laminated for him. He would pick up new maps at the outfitters. He knew the details constantly changed. Portages were redrawn. Old campsites were retired, and new ones needed to be broken in.

He would need to make some changes to his own map.

Several summers ago, a section of the area had burned out of control for days. The weather had been unusually dry, and lightning had struck. Smoke and ash carried for hundreds of miles. Justin had read that, while the outfitters had a sprinkling system that had saved their buildings, much of the nearby forest land had been consumed. Justin thought he remembered someone quoted as saying that the fire had been a natural occurrence, and therefore it had been allowed to burn unhindered for as long as it took to go out naturally.

COLIN

Although Colin brought his overnight bag, he wasn't planning to go anywhere. The drive to the airport was in heavy traffic and it took him over an hour. He intended to park in the remote lot, because it seemed the most anonymous, and it was always the cheapest option. He wasn't sure if there was a minimum stay required, but he would find that out soon enough.

And then he changed his plan.

He was certain that he had never noticed a sign offering rewards parking before. But this time he did see it. He followed the circuitous route to an underground location. He punched his temporary code number into a keypad at the entrance to the garage, and then once again at the door to a discreetly placed elevator, after he had abandoned his car.

The elevator door opened noiselessly only feet from the entrance to the rewards suite he had visited a few nights before.

He considered entering what he now liked to think of as his "lucky" numbers into the keypad on the wall, even though the gesture had previously proved pointless. Instead, he entered the four numbers of his allocated temporary code and gained admittance.

The interior of the rewards suite was once again muted and empty, and Colin, having recently shelled out a large sum to be deemed worthy of full membership, was not surprised.

Money buys silence.

He was careful to sit where he sat before. As before, he was smothered in a balm of soothing jazz music. This time a guitar and bass combination were playing what sounded to Colin very much like a James Bond theme.

He placed his overnight bag where it was visible. Did it look a little anemic? Could anyone tell that there was nothing inside it?

He requested a coffee from a young man he did not recall seeing on his previous visit. He was not asked for his card, or for his money, or for his number, and Colin now began to understand how it was for the rich. He would be debited extravagantly at the end of the month, and it would be impossible to purchase anything that would equal, much less exceed, this astronomical amount.

But that wasn't the point. Being rich meant being able to put a discreet distance between yourself and your money. It was there, but it was refined and rendered invisible.

He allocated less than a split second to look around.

Mr. Elliot Devine was not in the house tonight. The two gentlemen working the rewards suite did not look familiar. Colin recalled that his previous server had been a young woman wearing a Celtic cross necklace. There had also been a young man working that night.

Colin remembered a glass on the table in front of Devine. He thought it had been a whisky glass. Devine had been sitting smoking his cigar at the table closest to Colin. It would therefore make sense that they had both been served by the same woman.

What else did he remember about the woman who served him? He remembered the shortbread and the excellence of the coffee.

He had remembered the necklace because Ruby had owned a similar one, fashioned out of filigreed white gold. She had loved it. It was going to go to Tony now. Perhaps he would one day have a wife who would want to wear it.

His coffee arrived quickly, and once again came replete with a rectangle of lightly sugared shortbread.

Colin spoke up. "Thank you."

"You're welcome, sir."

"I was here a few nights ago."

"Then welcome back, sir."

Colin pressed on, "There was a young lady who served me. I was sitting right here. At this table. I was hoping to see her working here tonight."

Maybe it was because he hadn't asked a question. There was no response.

This was not going according to plan. The young woman was supposed to be working tonight. The young woman with the cross. The young woman who had served him before. He would show her a picture of Devine, at which she would eagerly nod her head and validate his every suspicion. Perhaps she would even remember his name. And not his old name. But his new name. The one he was using now that Mr. Elliot Devine was supposed to be dead.

Colin was forced to improvise.

"The thing is," he began hesitantly. "I hadn't remembered to tip her, and I wanted to make it up to her now."

This gambit received the thinnest of smiles. "She isn't here tonight, sir. You could leave it for her now. If you like." The offer was a frosty one.

Colin could feel the veneer of politeness about to be scraped thin.

He kept going. "Yes. I suppose I could. Could you perhaps tell me her name?"

Could he sound any more pathetic?

He received the answer he deserved. "I'm sorry, sir. I'm afraid I couldn't."

At this juncture, Colin paused. He could quit now, or he could reveal himself as a total creep. He could keep coming back here, but that would be creepier still. Or he could press harder for her name right now. If he had her name, he could probably find her. Angie could definitely find her. Still creepy. But marginally less creepy?

He made a fast decision. In a moment the creep spoke. "I thought she was very pretty."

Again, there was pained silence.

In desperation Colin opted for a robust display of man-to-man honesty. "I have to tell you: What I really wanted to do was ask her out."

There was more silence. Then Colin did something he had never done before. He placed five hundred dollars on the table, then waited. It was a short wait. The money was rapidly removed.

"Which night was this?"

Colin told him. He was, he sadly noted, no longer a sir.

"Her name is Linda Jackson."

Colin wanted to be sure.

"Does she wear a Celtic cross around her neck?"

There was an almost imperceptible nod.

He was out his dignity and five hundred bucks. Colin decided to push his luck. He pulled out a printout of Elliot Devine's likeness from the obituary notices.

"Have you ever seen this man here?"

The young man glanced at the piece of paper very quickly. When he spoke, it was in a neutral tone. "No."

"Would you tell me if you had?"

There was a suggestion of a pause. "Perhaps."

"I have more money."

If he had wanted to ask any more questions, he was too late. The young man walked away.

Colin quickly finished his coffee and got up to leave.

As he left the rewards suite, he contemplated how much damage he'd done to his newfound status as a rewards member.

He decided probably not that much. He'd revealed himself as a minor creep, given a bribe for a woman's name, and inquired after another rewards member who had been in the suite at the same time as he had. Showing the picture might be a tad odd, but his behavior was hardly cause for blackballing or loss of member privileges. And his gauche money had been accepted.

But, as he rode the elevator downward, Colin Tugdale felt unusually sleazy. The sensation lasted a while.

When the doors opened, he exited into the parking garage.

Colin called Angie. He had a name: Linda Jackson. She listened to him, and when he had finished speaking, she asked the obvious question.

"And now what will you do?"

He had blustered his response, "I'll find her. *We'll* find her," he quickly amended. "She'll confirm it. That he's still alive. That I saw him. That he's not dead."

"Then what?"

"I don't know."

"I do," she said. "We should track him down."

"How will we do that?"

"I don't know." She pretended to hesitate. "What do we know about him?"

"We know he's not dead."

He heard her sigh. "That's true. What else?"

"He smokes cigars. He tried to buy Trench Warfare from Tony. He failed. He likes to go camping."

"Good boy. And where does he like to camp?"

Colin wasn't sure how he felt about being patronized. But he played along.

"In the Frontier Waters."

"And where is that?" she wondered.

"It's way up north. Near Duluth."

"I believe you own property up that way," she mused.

"Why are we doing this?"

"Because we're nosy and we both think the answer is going to be interesting?"

"Why else?"

"You know why else. The scan and the weld," she began.

"What about them?"

"I want you to tell me the truth. Do you trust them?"

He wanted to ask what she meant. But he didn't. Because he knew exactly what she meant. Angie Rennie had cheated the weld and lived. Elliot Devine had probably done the same thing.

But first he had to find Linda Jackson.

JUSTIN

The walk through the city from the local bus stop to the interstate bus station took Justin ten minutes. He passed a bike shop and a craft brewery.

The interstate bus would leave in twenty-five minutes, heading north and terminating near the border. At the ticket office, Justin paid for his one-way ticket with the outer layers of his cash wad. He sat down inside the refurbished interior of the station. The waiting room was cold. He pulled the hood of his sweatshirt up over his head. His hair was cut very short, and he had shaved his face slowly and carefully that morning.

Justin planned to take the bus as far as Duluth and walk the rest of the way.

He had begun to follow the rules of his destination, to leave no trace.

A number of seats inside the bus station were occupied by homeless men charging their phones and dozing. One gentleman compulsively packed and unpacked three bags filled with his possessions. When he was finished he started over.

Justin watched him carefully. If there was a method, he was unable to identify it.

The other station users were young people, hipsters of both sexes, drinking large coffees purchased at the terminal coffee bar. Mostly the men talked, and the women worked on their laptops.

The hip young never stayed long. Bus numbers and routes were announced and they would get up and leave and be quickly replaced. The homeless men sat slumped motionless in their seats, occasionally checking the status of their phones as if they had a place they had to get to with some urgency.

An older policeman walked through the terminal, on his beat, his pace slowing as he came closer to the homeless people. But he didn't stop, and he spoke to no one.

Justin wondered if he swung back later in the day? And what would he do if the same homeless men were still there?

But by then Justin would be long gone.

COLIN

In the airport cell phone parking lot, Colin turned off the engine and left the key in the ignition.

On the tastefully muted airwaves of public radio, a frequent refrain aired, and Colin only half paid attention.

One of the hosts phrased the question: Has the Weld Really Made Us Well?

Most days, the wording got scrambled, even if the narrative tended to repeatedly loop back on itself. The perennial scab that the earnestly whispering cathode hosts never tired of picking was a compare/contrast lamentation on the nature of two societies: the worlds of pre- and post-Geneweld.

There was no question that, for better or worse, the post-weld planet was a changed place.

Patently self-evident, the following themes never ceased to draw professional pundits into earnestly revolving debate.

Very few old people were around.

The scan/weld technology was discovered during wartime, an apparently accidental stumble into genetic modification, as governments tinkered with ways to eradicate their enemies without resorting to traditional weaponry. The first generation of welds had all concluded at the turn of the new century, forever altering the world's demographic composition.

There were fewer doctors and nurses, medical schools and hospitals, and almost no hospices. No retirement communities nor nursing homes. Few companies made adult diapers or Viagra or motorized chairs that climbed up and down steep house stairs anymore.

Every one of these professions and products still existed, but in much smaller numbers.

Theoretically, the weld had been made available to every healthy person in every country in the world for the last forty years.

There were outlying religious/philosophical objections from people from all social strata, and there were people, more often wealthy people, who simply chose to opt out. Sometimes this went well; lives were lived both long and healthy, all the rigors of old age were relished, and a death long delayed came quickly and largely free of pain. But too often this choice went badly; when illness arrived, it was chronic and prolonged and financially devastating.

Most governments offered subsidized health care for those who failed the scan.

Occasionally the reverential voices at NPR waxed nostalgic for the rosy cheeked old-timers and the pearls of hard-earned wisdom passed lovingly down through the generations. But adult-onset dementia was virtually eradicated, sales of walkers plummeted, and the notion of retirement living was radically redefined.

People often chose to work on now, no longer slowing down mentally or becoming baffled into obsolescence by the demands of ever-changing technology. Those who did choose to retire, did so with a vengeance, scaling steep mountain faces, running competitively in marathons, staying up late, and never once playing bingo.

Scientifically, the weld remained something of a mystery. Julian Brand had been the scientist in charge of the original weld/scan research team. Brand, the "Weld Wizard," had been in his early thirties when the first apes were tested. He had famously chosen not to weld and had drowned at the disappointing age of fifty-eight on a remote camping trip. All the other original developers from the university in southern England were now concluded (they had unanimously opted to weld along with the first of the human volunteers, and they had all died at varying ages, all perfectly preserved, all almost exactly twenty years later).

The nature of conclusion was another area rife with mystery. What was understood was that, on a certain day, the heart simply stopped. Examples were studied, some were even documented, filmed, recorded, and poignantly preserved in real time.

For this seemingly peace-filled resolution, many let the concluding moment occur (as it were) naturally while others, anxious not to relinquish control, picked a moment and method of their own, before the reimagined and reformatted nature took its course.

But what to make of someone like Angie Rennie?

The history of the weld makes no mention of curative powers. But then, why should it? If scientists know anything about the weld, it is that the weld isn't about cure. The weld is about stasis. And for it to work it has to begin with a relatively clean medical slate.

As a research variable, several people with life-threatening diseases had been given the weld, very specifically, people with potent forms of terminal cancer. All had died well within the twenty years, all visibly aged, and most died from the cancer they originally had. A few did not. One pitiable young woman, having developed one type of cancer, rolled the dice and lost bigger, as a more virulent form seized her already-ravaged body, and propelled her faster to her end.

By this point Colin had listened to enough.

His laptop spat out a short list of all the Linda Jacksons, or rather, all the Linda Jacksons who lived within a reasonable commuting distance from the city airport.

He could resume sleuthing.

∞

It turned out that Linda Jackson had once been a very popular name.

That was the bad news.

But there were avenues of hope. As Colin discovered, most of the Linda Jacksons were post-weld older ones. A clearly pre-weld Linda Jackson had served him his first coffee and shortbread at the airport. Some of the Lindas lived several states away. Two Lindas lived in the city. They were both young; one was only ten years old.

Colin's search was made easier because the name Linda was a relic from another era. It would take a teen rock star or a royal baby named Linda to relaunch the brand.

Plus, the other city Linda looked initially promising. An address in an ambiguously gritty neighborhood on the lower west side of the city. A forty-minute drive to the airport if she used the expressway.

The only suburban age-appropriate Linda lived near the lake, in the near northern suburbs, only a half hour to and from the airport.

City Linda was ubiquitous on social media. She had a website filled with pictures of pastries and was wearing a white jacket and a chef's hat in most of her pictures. Her numerous friends were mostly women, and they all loved her confections, and Colin couldn't help but be a little surprised at how thin they all looked. They all praised a particular restaurant located two blocks from her apartment, where this Linda Jackson was listed as both a part owner and the pastry chef.

Colin was left with suburban Linda Jackson.

While the drive south from the airport would have been painless, the passage east across the suburbs toward the lake proved slower going. Colin drove aggressively and made it in just over an hour, stopping for gas, where he called Angie.

After he provided a progress report, Angie praised his detective work. She offered help. Then she had hung up on him.

Colin couldn't help but notice that Angie sounded distracted. But she promised she would call him back later.

Colin parked his car half a block east of the intersection where Linda Jackson's apartment building was located and awaited instructions.

As promised, Angie called back. She spoke quickly, "You're outside a store called Transmission."

"I am," he agreed. "They're having a shoe sale."

"That's very nice. They probably carry pumps in your size. You need to walk a block east. Go under the train tracks. On the left, there will be a coffee shop. Go there. You like coffee. Apparently, the cheesecake is wonderful. You should probably have some. Everyone loves the chocolate chip the best. They will put whipped cream on top if you ask nicely. Wait for her there."

"Can I have the cream on top?"

"It'll go straight to your hips."

"I've got less than two years to live."

"Have the cream."

He walked the block east, passing a secondhand record store, passing a hot dog stand with a laboriously cute name, passing a vegetarian restaurant discreetly accessed from an alleyway. A northbound commuter train rattled and sparked overhead.

The coffee shop was small, with machines hissing steam behind a counter and a mini labyrinth of whitewashed pine tables. Both the free weekly newspapers were available in vending machines chained up outside the front door. He carefully extracted a copy of each.

Colin balanced on a wobbly chair by the window. When he was relatively secure, he began to read.

The mayor of the big city was far from popular. The sanitation department leased a truck parking area on the north side that was going to be developed. More people were biking the city streets, and more bicyclists were getting killed in traffic accidents. Cyclists blamed drivers. Drivers blamed cyclists. The newspaper blamed the mayor. A cross-dressing man had his wife's permission to date other people. He wanted to know if he could also cross-dress on these dates. He was advised not to push his luck.

He had been sitting only five minutes before his coffee and cheesecake arrived. He had forgotten to ask for the cream, but there it was, squatting on top anyway. Apparently Angie didn't know everything.

Half an hour later, the young woman who had served his coffee and shortbread at the airport walked into the coffee shop.

She was dressed in gym shoes and baggy sweatpants and a loose, faded T-shirt. She sat down beside him.

They shook hands. Her handshake was firm.

"I'm Linda Jackson. And you're Colin. Your friend Angie contacted me. She told me what you're doing." She nodded slowly to herself. "I was wondering if I would remember you."

"And do you?" he asked her.

"I do." Linda Jackson seemed pleased. "It was quiet. You were the only upgrade there. Not a full member. You had that conflicted look the upgrades always have. Like you are ridiculously happy to be there, and you expect to be thrown out at any moment."

He laughed, "Was that really what I looked like?"

Her smile was mostly sympathetic. "I'm afraid so. Show me your picture."

He did, but she barely glanced at it. "Angie sent it to me already. I just wanted to make sure. She sent me the same picture. It's a little clearer on paper. I also wanted to be sure you are both who you say you are. That you are working together." She seemed convinced on all counts.

Colin asked, "Would you like something? It would be my pleasure."

She replied, "Did you have their cheesecake?"

He nodded ruefully toward his well-scraped plate.

She placed her finger on the picture of Elliot Devine on the table. She looked again at it quickly, and she nodded her head slowly.

"It's definitely him. He was there. The same night that you were. Sitting close to where you were sitting. He drank a single malt whisky. An Islay. A large one. He left a big tip."

Colin couldn't help but look bashful. Linda Jackson smiled at him. "No worries. Yours was just fine." Something in her choice of words convinced him that Devine's had been a whole lot bigger.

A coffee was placed in front of her. There had been no visible means of communication.

She hastened to explain, "They know me here. This is my laundry night. The machines are in the basement of our apartment building. The wash takes half an hour. I get myself a coffee. I go back. I put the clothes in the dryer. Another half hour. I come back here. I finish my coffee. I'm living the dream." She pointed to the picture. "Angie told me he's supposed to be dead."

"He is."

"Are you curious about why I'm meeting you."

"I just assumed that Angie was very persuasive?"

She gave a short laugh. "Oh, she is. I'll give you that. No. What you're doing here—what you two are both wondering— you see, I've had the same experience before. With another customer at work. At the airport one night. He looked so much like someone. Like someone I was certain was dead. I never figured out who he was. Or who he had been, I should say. But it was someone. I was sure of it then. I still am." There was a slight hesitation. "Oh, maybe not so much now. It's been a while. But I still think about it sometimes." She looked defiantly at Colin. "And you are sure about this one?"

"I am," he said. Colin pointed to the picture. "Do you remember his name?"

She shook her head sadly. "It doesn't work that way. You get in with your number. Sometimes people bring guests in. We don't bother to bill you for what you order. You pay your dues every month. As you know, it's a fortune. You can't possibly order enough stuff from us to come close to the amount you pay. You can tip us. With your credit card if you like. Or you can do it with cash." She paused, and she shook her head. "And I know just what you're going to ask next."

"He tipped you with cash."

Her shake became a wistful nod. "He did. Just like you did. And the truth is that most of our customers do. I suspect that wealth and the desire for anonymity often go hand in hand."

Colin was sure that was true.

"He might have been an upgrade like me."

She answered quickly, "He wasn't. I can always tell. He seemed at home."

"So not an upgrade?"

She smiled. "Very definitely not."

"So how do I find his name?"

Linda Jackson answered, "The only record of his being there is the keypad at the door that lets him in. He entered his number and inserted his card."

Colin knew that accessing the keypad records was well beyond his computing skills, but he wondered about Angie. He would ask her. If she wasn't working on it already.

Colin sat back. A southbound train rattled the plates and cups on the high shelves behind the counter. Linda Jackson sipped her coffee.

Colin said quietly, almost to himself, "I wonder if he was coming or going that night."

He wasn't expecting an answer but he got one: "He was going."

Colin was surprised. "You could tell that?"

She laughed. "Maybe I could," she considered the possibility for a moment. "But no. He made it a lot easier. He told me. He was going to Duluth, Minnesota.

"What time is it?" she asked.

Colin told her.

"I left my phone in the basement. It's almost time for the dryer."

"Thank you again for seeing me. For helping us."

"Did I help you?"

He assured her that she had.

Linda Jackson took her coffee to the counter where a thin young man nodded gravely to her and took it away. She came back to the table.

"Will you still be here when I get back?" she asked Colin.

He told her he wouldn't.

She wished him luck. Then she left.

Five minutes later, after Colin had placed a very large tip on the table, he left too.

JUSTIN

The interstate bus was fiercely air-conditioned and half empty. Justin had both seats to himself and he kept his hood pulled up for the length of the journey.

In Duluth he disembarked. It was early evening. The resale shop was the same one where all the kids had bought their flannels several years ago. It was open late. Justin found a used hoodie in his size. It was a pale grey. His old one was a pale blue. He handed the blue one over as a partial trade-in and was given a dollar credit. The new hoodie was five dollars. He used up more of his cash for the balance of the transaction.

Justin walked the length of the lake walk, killing time. He bought a chocolate malted and sat in the park to eat it. The breeze off the lake was cooler and the air temperature was dropping fast.

It was much later when Justin walked up the hill, away from the water, and across the church parking lot. It was the same church where they had stayed the last night after the canoe trip, before the long drive home. It was the same denomination as the church the campers attended. The associate pastor had let them in that night, welcomed them warmly, boasting that their church doors were never locked, that everyone would be made welcome. To Justin, he had sounded like he meant it.

The young man had insisted on shaking hands and introducing himself. His name was Jeffrey; they should call him Pastor Jeff.

Pastor Jeff had seemed like a good guy.

Outside the side entrance, Justin studied a notice board planted in the grass. Pastor Jeff was now the senior pastor.

The parking lot was deserted as Justin walked to the last line of empty spaces and looked down on the city. There were street lights below that demarcated the main thoroughfares that ran at right angles to each other. Further away, the shipyard cranes stood illuminated in geometric poses, shimmering against the dark of the distant lake water.

Justin remembered standing there watching the sunrise on the morning before they headed home.

He walked back across the lot and pulled the handle of the church door. Pastor Jeff was as good as his word; the door was unlocked.

Inside, the building was dark, and Justin navigated the hallway by the red glow of the exit signs. He found a meeting room with an ugly assortment of overstuffed chairs and couches and a badly scarred coffee table placed in the center.

He took his hoodie off and folded it carefully before placing it inside his bag. He pulled out his towel and wrapped it around his duffel. He lay down on the couch and placed his makeshift pillow under his head. The room was warm and stuffy.

Justin heard a tanker out in the channel blow its horn three times, then an answering sequence of bridge horns, then the quieter ringing sound, as the Aerial Lift Bridge rose vertically one hundred and forty feet in the air to allow the huge ship to pass safely through.

Justin thought about going over to the window to watch. But his thought was as far as he got. He was asleep before the bridge came back down and the street traffic could pass safely through.

∞

In the early morning Justin repacked his duffel. He washed his face in the church bathroom. He left some money in a collection envelope, which he found on top of a neat stack on a table right outside the church sanctuary.

Justin was walking across the parking lot as the first car pulled in. He hoped it might be Pastor Jeff, but the young man looked more custodial than pastoral. Justin smiled and the man smiled back as he pulled two buckets filled with cleaning supplies from the back of his car.

The final part of his journey was a nearly twenty-hour trek on paved trail along the north shore of the lake, a few detours on backroads inland, a stretch or two of gravel pathway, and then a section of gravel road proper, as he left the shoreline and headed northwest toward the outfitters.

From the start, Justin walked the trail with purpose. When he stopped once to throw himself in the lake, it took his breath away. As he swam, he drank, although there were water fountains close to habitation, and streams to drink from as he walked the more remote portions of the trail.

Justin passed several small towns, and he ate his meals at cafés along the trail that catered to hikers and bicyclists. He wore a T-shirt and shorts with his wool socks and sturdy shoes, which were technically made for water but doubled as hiking boots. At Two Harbors, he drank his coffee at a coffee shop in a bike store. He bought a baseball cap that featured the bike store logo.

Justin had spent a lot of time thinking about traveling unobtrusively, about leaving no trace. His duffle bag had adjustable straps that made it easy and comfortable to carry on his back. He had packed his bag carefully. It was perfectly balanced. He would look a little dirty and unshaven in a day or two, but in a day or two everyone else around him would look pretty much the same.

He estimated that the trip would require him to sleep unsheltered for just one night if he made good time on the first day.

Walking fast, he considered his bedtime options.

He would look worn and out of place and conspicuously vehicle-less in a roadside motel. He had no camping supplies for an overnight stay at a state park.

This one night was the most problematic. Once he got to his destination, he could begin to improvise. He could begin to disappear.

He passed a sign on the trail and he stopped. He read it twice. The second time to make sure, because he could not believe what he was reading.

TÖFTEHÖSTEL

The latest venture from Zack Todd, media entrepreneur and visionary

TÖFTEHÖSTEL. *A Eurasian-style hostel for backpackers, for bikers, for urban bohemians. A place for hardcore souls who thrive on a little discomfort. A place for organic souls who could use saving a little scratch for beer and adventure and life's other essentials. A place at the end of the day, for tired souls to unwind, to recharge after a long day's interface with Mother Nature.*

Justin didn't read all this at first; he stared uncomprehendingly at the first word for several seconds, wondering what TÖFTEHÖSTEL meant, wondering how to pronounce TÖFTEHÖSTEL, which came liberally doused with umlauts. Much later he would be able to more fully digest the hyperbolic puffery on one of several conveniently located laptops running superfast Wi-Fi and offered gratis.

TÖFTEHÖSTEL was an abandoned hardware store, Ikea-ized with dorm-style rooms on the first floor and communal showers and toilets on the second. Twenty dollars cash got you a bunk bed, enclosed on three sides, with storage lockers underneath. It was quiet, and Justin had the choice of a top or bottom bunk in a building that housed forty people and boasted a walkout deck, kitchenette areas, and an indoor sitting area for chilly nights.

Justin took a long shower and padded downstairs to his bunk, barefoot and wrapped in a fluffy towel.

Early the next morning, he hiked away from the lake toward the outfitters, with more than ten miles to go. It would take three hours if he followed the trail, slightly longer if he kept off the gravel as much as possible.

COLIN

It hadn't initially occurred to Colin to invite Angie Rennie up north for what he privately referred to as the ceremony of the ashes, part two.

It had been four days since he had seen her in person. He had cried then. It had been two days since he had spoken to her, two days since he had met with Linda Jackson.

Before he left the northern suburbs, he called Angie and told her everything Linda Jackson had said. She mostly listened. She asked about the cheesecake. He had perversely told her it was foul. She asked if Linda had worn the Celtic cross, and he admitted that he hadn't noticed.

Then he asked her about going to the cottage with him, and she said yes.

The cottage wasn't far from Duluth. Elliot Devine had flown to Duluth. The Natural Boundary Foundation had a post office box in Duluth, and Duluth was on the way to the Frontier Waters, where the NBF and Devine found pretty photographs to decorate their websites.

All roads were leading to Duluth.

Not for the first time, Colin wondered if he was dating or detecting. Maybe a little of both, he thought. He wondered if Angie felt the same. He hoped so.

Colin had remembered to stop his mail and his newspaper delivery. He had asked the youngsters next door to watch the house, and while they assured him that they would, he wasn't optimistic.

When he wasn't settling his affairs before traveling, Colin thought about what Linda Jackson had said. She confirmed that Elliot Devine, the not dead and clearly not dearly departed Elliot Devine, was the man he had seen at the airport lounge, sipping his whisky in the enveloping dark of the private room, smoking his cigar, and tipping like a bigshot before taking a flight north to Duluth.

The reason Linda Jackson had proved helpful was her conviction that she, too, had encountered a person she had every reason to believe should be dead.

Colin carefully read the newspaper each morning. It was the largest national paper in the country, and it was faithfully delivered to his house seven days a week.

On the day before he left town, there was an article buried in a middle section about people who vanished. The article referred to them as the Disappeared, and they were legion. The Disappeared were mostly ordinary people, who were not in trouble, not in debt, not wanted by the police, nor were they especially unloved or unwanted. The article used the term *marginalized*, which Colin considered to be negative. They left neatly and carefully; they had planned ahead, their bills paid before they vanished, dishes washed, milk and other perishables taken out of the fridge. Their cars were paid for and abandoned in places where it would take a while for them to be noticed.

They almost never came back. Bodies were seldom dis-covered mangled in sad and desolate places. Cash in bank accounts stayed where it was, although sometimes family members needing help received anonymous funds by wire. Fake IDs were easy to procure, and the police weren't terribly interested, if there wasn't any suspicion of a crime.

It was assumed that they led new lives. Several experts believed that they simply recreated the minutiae of their previous existence elsewhere. If they washed dishes in a restaurant in one town, they likely now washed dishes in a restaurant in another town.

But other experts thought that a dramatic break was more likely. A drastic new life. Perhaps in a dream town they had read about, or a favorite vacation spot remembered from childhood.

If they had been single, they might now choose to marry.

All the experts agreed that the Disappeared would try to find a place where they could feel love.

Colin tried to slot Elliot Devine into the ranks of the Disappeared. If Devine was running, he was running from a tangible threat of six people, all blonde, plus lawyers, all after his money. It was possible that he was dead, and that Colin had been mistaken. But it was also possible that he had faked his own conclusion. Colin supposed it could be done, although he also strongly suspected that Devine had too much money to find true anonymity.

Colin finished the article just as Angie texted him. The texts became an electronic flurry.

She was coming over.

He told her he would pick her up.

She asked when.

In an hour.

She told him she had packed already.

He said that was great.

She reminded him they hadn't decided how long they would stay.

Was that okay?

Yes. She was flexible.

He had also already packed, and this he did not share in a text.

For the next hour, Colin invented a number of small things to do around his house. And as he killed time, he found that he couldn't stop smiling.

He loved his cottage. He was bringing a date. He was going to sprinkle his dead wife's ashes on the water. He was chasing the trail of a dead man.

A favorite location. A possible new romance. A sad occasion. A sense of adventure.

He was at Angie's front door in just under an hour and a half. They were on the road and heading north ten minutes later.

There had been no doorbell for Colin to ring. Instead there was a section of brittle, unpainted wood forming the silhouetted outline of where a doorbell had once been. The front door itself was tiger striped, with peeling paint and untreated veneer, weather abused, visibly buckled in places. The blades of grass out front were sparse enough to be individually countable, and Colin could see no evidence of even the most cursory yard care.

Behind a leaf-encrusted screen, a window curtain parted seconds after his knock. The front door opened, and, a moment later, a decidedly curious Colin was ushered silently across the shabby threshold.

"Welcome."

The interior of Angie's house was small and bright and immaculate as a new pin. Period wood tables supported an explosion of freshly cut flowers. A cheerful mélange of antique rugs spread across slickly polished oak floors, the pristine wood surfaces extending across and upwards, merging organically into the carved door frames and the staircase.

Colin continued to look around. "I'm assuming you didn't tidy the place for me."

"You would be correct in that assumption."

"All these flowers didn't come from the garden."

"There's a flower stand in the summer months between the train station and the Mexican restaurant.

Colin knew it well. He had shopped there himself on occasion. "They're very pretty."

"Why thank you. I love flowers."

"I assume you don't care much for tending them."

Her smile was mysterious. "Why do you think that?"

"Well," he faltered, "your yard—"

"—Is an illusion I'm happy to provide."

She had already packed her small shoulder bag, and it lay at her feet. An immense pale grey sweatshirt was draped across her shoulders.

He proceeded hesitantly, "The inside and the outside of your house. They don't—"

"No, they don't. I live on the inside. The outside is a deception."

He was barely able to stop himself from remarking on the effectiveness of the deception.

Minutes later, as Colin pointed his car in a northerly direction over empty roads, Angie sat motionless in the soft leather of the passenger seat, cocooning herself in the expanse of her sweatshirt.

"I get cold when I'm nervous," she offered.

A vintage white plastic Apple laptop was perched on Angie's lap. Their bags nestled together on the back seat. Approximately half of Ruby Tugdale's ashes wedged securely between the two bags.

Angie finally asked, "Where will you put them?"

"Somewhere," he told her. "By the edge of the water. I'm not sure yet."

But Colin was being evasive. He had a plan. He would row one of their two kayaks out into the lake. There was a raft a hundred feet from the shore that they used to swim out to. In the interests of strict verisimilitude, Colin should have swum out to the raft holding onto the ashes. In his mind's eye, he imagined this very scene, an Olympian tableau, where an urn was brandished above the waves by a godlike creature swimming with effortless strokes across the smooth water.

But that didn't seem a practical notion. He wasn't that strong a swimmer. His half-baked plan was to paddle the distance then stand on the raft and throw the ashes into the air. He prayed he wouldn't spill most of Ruby inside the canoe on the way out there.

"Where did you put the rest of her ashes?" Angie asked him.

"In the garden. In amongst her flower beds. It was what she wanted."

"We have that in common."

"What's that?"

"We both find comfort in flowers."

He stopped at a four-way intersection.

"Make a right here," she told him.

"The highway is the other direction," he was quick to point out.

"I know," she said.

The laptop was open, and Angie was typing.

"The drive is going to take us most of the day."

She didn't look up. "Are we in a hurry?"

He turned right as he was instructed.

A few minutes later she looked up from the screen and asked, "What are you thinking about?"

His stated answer was nothing. But the unspoken answer was the raft, and the lake. And it was also Ruby.

The very first thing Ruby Tugdale did when she got to the cottage for the season was to run from the car to the water and throw herself headfirst into the lake. It was in the late spring when her breathless first plunge took place, initiating what would be her daily ritual. Ruby swam first thing in the morning and at sunset every day at the cottage, rain or shine, mostly alone in the morning, usually accompanied by Colin at dusk, as the season progressed.

The end of the drive north usually came at exactly the right time in the day for her ritual to commence.

On the morning of the last day, she staged the final immersion, in the cooling lake water, as fall threatened, and the Tugdales reluctantly dragged themselves back to the city.

Her last plunge was carefully orchestrated. Her clothes and her shoes and her towel were all placed in the car beforehand, a plastic bag for her swimsuit lay ready. She would run from the water to the car. Then they would drive, and, by the time they stopped for coffee and gas an hour later, she would be dry and changed and sad as they bid farewell to the lake and the cottage.

Colin recalled the particulars of the last mile of the drive up north at the start of the season. Ruby would be excited; getting her keys and her wallet out of her pockets, putting them in the glove compartment, pulling off her shoes and socks. She wore her swimsuit under her clothes, and this would be revealed as the car came to a stop, the tires coming to rest deep inside the expanse of wild clover flourishing outside the beach house.

For the first few weeks, Ruby's two daily immersions were taken alone, the lake water proving too cold for Colin and, in his considered opinion, for anyone else possessed of warm blood and an aversion to hypothermia.

When Colin spoke again, he changed the subject. "That's a very old laptop."

She shook her head. "No, it isn't."

Colin persisted, "It looks old."

Angie smiled at him. "It's supposed to look old. It's got the newest and fastest processor you can buy. The memory is probably twenty times greater than the machine originally had. There are all kinds of passwords and encryption software loaded. It uses a lot of disk space because most of the data on it isn't something I want stored on any cloud. The graphics are terrible, but I can live with that. I'm not doing any gaming on this thing. This is my real computer."

"What do you play games on?"

"My shiny, brand-new computer."

"Did you bring your brand-new computer?"

She shook her head. "That would be difficult."

"Why?"

"Because someone broke into my house and stole it."

He had a feeling he knew the answer to his next question before he asked it. But he asked it anyway.

"What else was taken?"

"Nothing else was taken."

"Nothing?"

"Except for my diamond tiara and my collection of sketches by Picasso."

As Colin continued to drive north, Angie Rennie explained her system. She told him that she painstakingly updated the hardware innards of her old computer every year. She changed the passwords twice weekly. She also bought herself a new model every year.

He wondered aloud what she kept on the new models.

"An elaborate puzzle of outright lies. A collection of bogus information. Files filled with fake passwords and spreadsheets filled with financial information on companies that don't exist. Foreign bank accounts in mythical places with invented currencies. I even have money in an offshore account in the Bank of Galma."

"Where's that?" he asked.

"It's an island in Narnia," she laughed. "All this fake stuff is fake protected. It's a balance between being not too easy to decipher and not too hard to decipher. A challenge. But a solvable challenge.

"There are two types of thief: the thief who wants a computer and anything else he can get his hands on, and the thief who wants *my* computer. The first type of thief will scrub the hard drive and sell the new machine, and that's fine because scrubbing the drive and giving the new machine to a charity shop is all I ever do with it anyway. The second type of thief will be able to access all the fake information, and that's fine, too. They'll just find a bunch of stuff I want them to find."

He asked who she thought took it. Which kind of thief?

"That's a good question. I'm going to go with the second thief. Nothing else was taken. I don't have a whole lot, but I have an antique German camera that's about the most valuable thing I own. It was on the shelf, in clear view. Right beside the computer. It's still sitting there. I've bought some expensive jewelry over the years that I don't often wear. It was sitting in an open box near the computer. It also wasn't touched. The camera and the jewelry are my tests. So, I don't really know. Nothing much was messed up. They were only in the house for a short time. I walked to the flower shop that afternoon. I was gone an hour. They must have been watching the house."

He remembered something. "When I called you about Linda Jackson . . ."

She nodded her head. "I'd just got back home."

"You sounded a little distracted."

"I'm sure I was. The front door was skillfully picked. I always lock it and it's a decent bolt. No one seemed to have looked very hard for anything else. So, it was the second thief. They wanted my computer. They got the wrong one."

"So, you keep the new computer near the camera and the jewelry on purpose?"

She nodded.

"Where was the old computer?"

"In an old cardboard box in a closet. Beside a BlackBerry and an abandoned answering machine."

"That's very clever," he admitted.

"Thank you." She was growing distracted.

"What are you thinking now?"

"I'm thinking that there's a third kind of thief."

"What kind is that?"

"That's the kind of thief who would have spent less than five minutes with the new computer then torn the house apart till they found the older one."

"But that wasn't the thief who broke in."

"No," she admitted with a tight smile. "I'm happy to say that this time it wasn't." There was a long pause. "What time were you in the rewards lounge?"

"Which time?"

"The first time. Which night was that?"

He thought for a moment, then told her.

He noticed that she typed very quickly as he continued to drive.

"There were three more flights that night to Duluth," she told him.

"I'm guessing Elliot Devine wasn't on any of them."

"Oh, he was," she said. "He just wasn't calling himself Elliot Devine."

The typing resumed. Then it stopped again.

"A total of nine rewards customers flew on these three flights. I'm guessing that Devine flew on the first flight, right after he left the lounge." She stopped talking. She kept typing. "Four rewards customers were on that first flight. Damn." She looked annoyed.

"What is it?"

"I can't get the names of the people on these flights. But I can check hotel reservations. And I can check car rentals."

He was curious. "How many hotels are in Duluth?"

"Fifty."

"Car rentals?"

"Ten."

"We don't know his name."

She could only nod her head in agreement.

"Do you know what I'm thinking? I'm thinking that the timing of all this is very interesting. I'm having my credit checked for no good reason by a credit company I've never heard of. I'm being robbed. I don't generally get robbed. The outside of my house discourages people interested in getting their hands on fancy stuff."

"And you're worried?"

"No," she allowed at last. "I'd have to say I'm really more curious than worried. They took nothing but my computer. They didn't take the interesting computer. They took nothing else. So, I should assume they wanted my computer. But they weren't clever enough to find the right one. Or even to look for the right one. Or perhaps not." She looked thoughtful.

"What else are you thinking?"

"I think I'm being given a warning. Or two warnings. And I'm thinking it's a good time for me to leave town. I think my warnings are only moderate ones. They could have given me a more serious one."

"Moderate warnings?"

"Yes, I think so."

"Why?"

"I'm annoying someone."

"No, I mean, why is it a moderate one?"

She stopped typing and held up her laptop. "Because if they'd taken this computer I would have been really worried."

"Who is doing this?'

She shrugged. "I don't know for sure. But it's clearly your fault."

"And why is that?"

"Because it's all happened since I threw myself at you."

"Possibly just a coincidence."

"Oh, I doubt that."

"I must be bad luck."

"You must be."

Colin changed the subject. "You made me change direction back there. Are we being followed?" He sounded like a little kid.

"I've no idea," she said. "We might be."

"An evasive maneuver just in case?"

Angie shook her head in a display of mock sadness. "A neighborhood street festival in honor of beer and bratwurst."

"I see." He was momentarily deflated.

"Now it's your turn to look thoughtful."

"Maybe you're right. Maybe these things are connected. I mean, connected with you meeting me. I'm causing you trouble."

"Perhaps you are."

"Why is it you and not me?"

"Why is there no credit check for you? Why is there no one breaking into your house? It's possible that you did get a check, and you just don't know it, yet. But I'm guessing you didn't. And no one broke into your house. I think you would have noticed that. Think for a moment about what we've done. And try to focus on the traceable stuff. Your wife is dead. You buy a fancy plane ticket. You like it so much you sign up for more fancy tickets. You go to a fancy place and drink coffee. You visit a website for a nature group."

He interrupted her there. "I made a donation."

She laughed. "Good. That's a perfect reason. There's a connection between the fancy club and the website. And that connection is Devine. But I defy anyone to spot it based solely on what you were doing. You asked some strange questions at the fancy place. You visited a woman who works there. Unless someone is following you, none of this stuff shows up as a paper trail. Or a digital one. Or an internet one. And now you're driving up north to visit a house you own."

"Have I made any mistakes so far?"

She was quick to burst his bubble. "Two."

"The first one?"

"You searched for Devine on the internet."

"And the second?"

"You're hanging around with me."

"You're a mistake?"

"I am. And I've made a few of my own. I ran a credit check on Natural Boundary. I've looked for Devine on the internet in a much more sustained way than you did. And then there's the fact that I am who I am."

"What do you mean?"

Her smile was empty. "What do I mean? I'm a career computer criminal and I'm annoying someone. You're a retired old man grieving for his lost wife. You're going to die soon. So how much harm can you cause? I've got plenty more years of making trouble left."

He should have been offended, but he wasn't.

"So, what are you doing that's causing all the trouble?"

"My first guess is annoying the NBF. The credit check woke them up. Then they saw me look for Elliot Devine. They credit checked me back. I'm sure of it."

"And the theft?'

"I think that was them, too. Another form of warning. And there's other stuff. The NBF website. I went there. And even now. I just ran a bunch of airline passenger searches for Devine on the night you saw him. I just ran a search of planes to Duluth that same night. The only address we have for the foundation is one in Duluth. I'm making it worse as we speak."

She took a deep breath before she continued.

"I've got to admit, I'm surprised that I got anyone's attention. My searches are well protected. I route them through dummy servers spread out across the world. But someone still managed to notice me."

"You think the foundation?"

She nodded. "They seem both protective and technologically savvy. It's not a pleasant combination."

They sat in silence for several minutes, while they both contemplated the ominous ramifications of Angie's cyber visibility.

"Which town is your cottage in?"

Colin looked a little sheepish. "It isn't—there really isn't much of a town. There's an excellent organic food store. Their prices are cheaper than regular supermarkets in the city. There's a gas station with overpriced premium and bad coffee. And Sal's Snug Roadhouse, on the next lake over, does a great panfried walleye dinner special on a Friday night in the summer. There are lots of fish in our lake. They keep it well stocked. But not with walleye, for some reason. There's easy access to canoeing and camping on national forest land, which is close by. A good hiking trail runs all the way down to the big lake."

"How's the internet service up there?"

"It used to be dismal."

"What happened?"

Colin smiled. "Tony visited and he made it much better."

"How far is Duluth from your place?"

"Maybe a hundred miles west, if you go the fastest way. It's a little slower, but much prettier, if you follow along the edge of the big lake."

"Can you drive any faster?"

"I certainly can."

She raised her eyebrows encouragingly.

Minutes later they arrived at the on-ramp for the expressway that headed north away from the city. There was a stoplight. He duly stopped on red. But as the light changed to green and Colin turned the corner, he stabbed his foot down on the accelerator. The six-cylinder engine lagged for a split second before two living people, their sparse collection of luggage, and the remaining remains of one dead person catapulted across three lanes of loitering trucks in a heedless rush.

After a few hours of driving, they stopped, wolfing down formidable sandwich creations at a fake castle dedicated to state-centric tourism and cheese. When the bill arrived, Angie snatched it up and paid quickly with two twenties at the cash register positioned by the door.

At the ATM outside, Angie suggested that Colin load up on cash, and he did just as he was told.

Later, they bought their groceries at the aforementioned organic food market, where they had intended to shop lightly, but the surfeit of bargains encouraged indulgence. Colin pulled out his credit card at the checkout, but Angie stepped in with a thick roll of paper currency and forked a great wad of it over before he could articulate a protest.

Colin found his voice outside in the parking lot. "I would have been happy to pay."

She turned on him, "Didn't I tell you to get cash?"

"I did."

"Good. Then what are you waiting for?" she said. She didn't wait for his answer. "You need to start using it."

"I assumed it was for emergency use."

"Well, it isn't."

"I can see that, now," he huffed.

"We need to make our movements a little harder to follow up here," she told him as they walked back to the car with their provisions. "We can't leave so much of a trail."

He got it.

JUSTIN

Justin arrived at Lauder Lake Outfitters in the middle of a Monday morning. He had remembered that Mondays were the turnaround day. Hundreds of campers, novices mostly, young adults and younger kids grumbling and kissing internet service and their phones goodbye. Unattended Duluth packs littering the paths to the waterfront landing, where a bottleneck of canoers waited to enter the waters. Others paddling across the last stretch of Lauder Lake before getting a welcome hot shower, turning in their rental equipment and canoes, and heading into town to blow their refunded deposit money on pizza, craft beer, and gourmet coffee.

Justin watched the comings and goings of canoes and bags and paddles and people.

He found an empty restroom inside the outfitters. He washed his hands and face and changed into his swim shorts. He took off his wool socks and packed them away. He kept his new baseball cap on.

The outfitters carried a range of inexpensive goods, with a decided bias toward the kind of items that people forget to pack. Justin had brought all his toiletries, but he had forgotten the white biodegradable soap that the outfitters stocked and recommended.

He bought a bar and picked up two new maps.

Sitting on the outside porch, he packed all three items away.

A wet nose was suddenly thrust into his lap.

Ten years ago, there had been a one-eyed golden retriever puppy at the outfitters. It still had one eye, but it was no longer a puppy.

A dirt road led to the other point of entry, a few miles north, the one on Selkirk Lake, the one his group had accessed by the short and bumpy truck ride, their Kevlar canoes secured to the trailers. This time, Justin planned to put in at Lauder Lake with everyone else.

As he had expected, at the landing the bags and boats and campers formed a dense unruly blockade of welcoming chaos. Justin soon spotted an orphan Duluth pack propped against a tree trunk. He gave it five minutes to be claimed before he moved in. He grabbed the bag. It was three-quarters full. Perfect. He opened the top, threw his duffle inside, closed it back up, and began to walk purposefully toward the mob at the edge of the water, all the while shouldering his newfound burden like he was born to it.

Stupidity was on display at the landing that morning. One canoe had tipped over. Someone was trying to climb into a boat while holding an open beer and a guitar. Paddles were misplaced, small children and large pets as well. Maps were hastily, belatedly, being consulted.

Justin had no need of his maps at this point; he had spent long hours consulting area websites, studying which individual campsites were popular, which were the most remote, which portages were the best maintained, where to hike, where not to hunt, which portages were almost but not quite abandoned, which lakes had the best fishing, calculating how far he could travel in a day, in a canoe, and on foot, especially on foot.

Paddling a canoe alone was a cumbersome chore. Carrying a canoe and a Duluth pack across a long portage wasn't easy. These two challenges he'd have to meet very soon. Carrying two bags strapped onto your chest and your back while balancing a boat on your shoulders was reserved for the very youngest and fittest; it was not something he planned to do.

Justin threw his newfound pack to the ground and sat down beside it. He had moved far enough away from the spot where the pack had first been abandoned. He felt safe enough. All the packs looked exactly the same. He wondered what was in it.

Justin pretended to be waiting. Several people talked to him. He made a show of looking exasperated and explained that the rest of his party were late. No one looked surprised at his explanation. Campers arrived and campers departed.

A sign tacked to a tree warned that phones would soon be useless, that service would vanish a short distance from the outfitters.

Justin wasn't concerned. His phone was lying on the kitchen table in his apartment. It was turned off, and his service was canceled.

He waited half an hour, until he saw that a canoe sat unmistakably abandoned. It had two paddles wedged inside. It was a nice Kevlar one, newish and beckoning and the brightest of yellows. From its positioning, Justin guessed that it had been brought back by campers unaware that they were required to carry it up the hill to the outfitters, where it could be inventoried, hosed down, and made ready for the next round of renters.

There was no sign of a life jacket inside. He sighed inwardly.

The outfitters staff would come for it at some point, either soon, or at the end of the busy day. The staff wore olive-colored polo shirts and affected a laid-back yet authoritarian manner. He looked around and saw no one fitting the description.

Casually, Justin walked over and picked it up. God, he had forgotten how light the Kevlar was. He gently placed it in the water, put his stolen bag in the center of the craft and climbed in; kneeling, he paddled slowly away from the melee, with bated breath and a steady stroke.

COLIN

At the cottage, Colin parked the car out front and carried the bags inside. Angie walked to the side of the house and across the clover-covered lawn, which descended all the way down to the lake. A metal dock spanned the sand and out into the water. She walked out onto it and stood, motionless, at the farthest end of the dock, her eyes tracking a family of ducks as they swam past her and then made their way out toward the raft.

There was the sound of the glass door sliding open. Footsteps tracking on the treated cedar wood. The noise unnaturally amplified and isolated by the absence of any other sound.

Then Angie could plainly hear the sound of water running in the kitchen.

Moments later, Colin called her name from the deck on the back of the house, and Angie turned around toward the sound of his voice.

"Do you want to swim?" His voice carried easily.

"Are you going to?" she called back.

"I think so."

"Is this the time for the ceremony?"

"Later . . . or tomorrow. Just a swim for now."

"Then I'm coming, too."

"Good," he said.

Ten minutes later, they entered the water.

The temperature was midsummer warm, as they swam in silence. Angie turned out to be about as average a swimmer as Colin was, and he was inexplicably pleased to make this discovery.

After they swam and dried off and put on fresh clothes, Colin prepared a meal of red beans, shrimp, and white rice, with green and yellow peppers and spicy andouille sausage. They had bought fresh bread from the organic market. Angie sat on the deck and listened to the lake through the tall trees. The glass door was open. The screen was pulled shut. There was a stiffening breeze and no sign of insects.

The water had been flat while they swam, but now tiny waves were pattering on the wet sand and against the metal deck supports.

"Do you have loons on your lake?" she asked him.

"There are two couples. They come each spring from Florida. Sometimes they get here too early, and the lake is still ice."

"What do they do?"

"They get a hotel room."

She snorted.

"I think they fly back south a way till they find water they can land on. I'm not sure. When the ice melts, they come back. And then they breed here. There's no natural island on the lake. We made one for them. It's very small. They usually have just one or two babies."

"Can you hear them sometimes?"

Colin told her that he often hears them in the darkness.

After a minute, she said, "Most of your trees look the same."

He answered from the kitchen, "Eastern hemlock."

"They're very tall. And straight. I like them."

"They can survive without much sunlight."

"Really?"

"Really."

"Are they old?"

"The taller ones are."

"How old?"

"Two hundred and fifty years old."

"Do they burn well?"

"Not especially. They're softwood."

"What do you use them for?"

"Deer use them for shelter in the winter."

"Anything else?" she asked.

"Poison."

"That's interesting."

"Socrates used hemlock to kill himself."

"Is that true?"

He hesitated. "Sort of," he said. "Actually, not really. Poison hemlock is a plant. Part of the carrot family. It's a poisonous plant that grows in Greece. Socrates was Greek. He probably used that."

"And your trees?"

"Not poisonous and not grown anywhere near Greece."

"I see," she said.

"Dinner is ready. We can eat it out here. We have some wine."

"What kind of wine?"

"The kind of wine that doesn't cost much and comes from New Zealand."

"Do you know much about wine?"

He barked out a laugh in response. "Almost nothing."

They ate on the deck with their plates in their laps and the wine glasses on the deck floor.

"I can cook about ten things," Colin informed her proudly.

"This is very good."

He looked sheepish. "It's probably my best."

"What do you call it?"

"Rice and beans with shrimp and sausage."

"That's certainly descriptive."

"Thank you. Can you cook?"

"I can make about five things. None as good as this."

He paused and pretended to consider. "So, we can survive for about two weeks."

Angie's mouth was still mostly full; she was obliged to nod her agreement.

∞

It was colder the next morning, and a mist spread across the stillness of the lake. Yesterday's breeze was stifled.

Colin paddled the kayak carefully toward the raft with Ruby's ashes wedged between his feet. His progress was slow and measured.

It was just after seven. The sun was up. Angie wasn't yet stirring. Colin couldn't say whether she was awake or not. He had made coffee and then left it to sit in the kitchen. They had slept in separate rooms, although there had been an emotionally fraught silence at the end of their dinner, when Colin thought the logistics of the evening might easily have been rearranged. But then they hadn't.

He dwelled on this as he rowed, aware that contemplating seduction and disposing of a deceased spouse's remains shouldn't be a simultaneous endeavor. Yet, they were.

It was difficult to lift the urn onto the raft, but somehow, by using the steps to pull himself up first, he managed. When he and the ashes were both secure he dragged the kayak up last.

The urn was still surprisingly heavy, and the lid was damp and tight and proved hard to open. He imagined spilling the contents all over the raft, and he suspected that Ruby would have laughed at him if he had.

Finally, the lid loosened, and he opened it.

Colin Tugdale sat on the edge of the raft with the urn in his hands as he began to speak.

"You told me to do something new. So, I am. It's an adventure."

He started to scatter the soot-grey flakes on the water.

"I'm scared for several reasons. And I miss you. I wish I had been older than you."

Colin began to cry.

"Goodbye, Ruby."

Even though his last two words were little more than a splutter and a whisper, they still reached across the water.

The urn was empty. He looked back toward the cottage, where Angie stood on the deck.

He knew she was watching him, although he was unable to see her face clearly.

If he had, he would have observed that she was also crying.

The sound of the first gunshot echoed across the silence.

JUSTIN

Justin sat down on the unmistakable remnants of a firepit with his plundered bag. He had crossed two lakes (Lauder and Goose) and two official portages (eighteen and forty-two rods, respectively) and made a hard hike (while it was not mapped, Justin mentally called out each rod as he walked, and his count was close to three hundred). He had found exactly what he was looking for: an abandoned campsite, not currently mapped but clearly identified on his older map, before the shifting topography had redrawn the shoreline of Goose Lake.

He stowed the canoe out of sight. The pack would be the first of many he would purloin, ransack, and return. He would sometimes get lucky and other times strike out. Tents and provisions and cooking gear were welcome booty; duffels crammed with teddy bears, Disney jammies, flip-flops, and teenage angst-riddled journals were a burden to be returned.

With a silent prayer, he opened his first bag.

His opening acquisition was something of a mixed bag. He spread out the contents. He had ropes and tarps (which were good) and a portable stove with extra oil and a jumbo box of matches (very good), but no food to cook (not so good). He soon discovered that he needn't have bought soap. He had an extra toothpaste, a new red toothbrush, a Harry Potter paperback, and a deodorant smelling of lavender. The deodorant and the *Goblet of Fire* would be returned—put in the bag to be swapped for another at the next busy portage. He had bug repellent and sunscreen (both good), a red fluffy beach towel (good), a Nalgene water container (good), and a two-piece black swimsuit (not good, not his size, and not a keeper). He strongly suspected that the faded jean cutoffs would also prove snug. Inside the pack of unknown origin, he also found contraband: a huge Ziploc bag filled with a trail mix of peanuts and pretzels and chocolate candies and raisins.

Cindy's name was Sharpied in large black print on the goodie bag.

He found Cindy's sundry other supplies: a week's worth of navy-blue bras and panties and a plastic container with a retainer inside.

He packed the food with all the clothes and other not good items back inside the pack. Then he tied a small rock to one of the ropes and threw it up and over a tree branch. When the stone returned to earth, he attached the pack to the rope and hoisted it twenty feet into the air before tying it off. This was to be the first of many nightly anti-bear measures.

The next thing he did was to use his tarps and his ropes to construct a shelter for the night.

When he was done constructing, he traced his steps back to Goose Lake. The water was warm near the shore. He swam far out before he would permit himself to drink and fill the Nalgene, and after that he lay back and pissed in the selfsame water. Back at the sandy shoreline, he broke out one of his new soaps, washed himself, and walked back to the campsite wrapped in his new fluffy red towel.

Once he was back at the camp, he lowered the pack and removed the trail mix.

It was far from a perfect meal, but Justin was hungry. After he finished eating, he used the water in the Nalgene to drink and brush his teeth. He wrapped himself up in the towel and lay down on the ground. He planned to sleep that night in his hoodie, his wool socks, and a change of underwear.

It was a warm night. There was a breeze, but he still applied bug repellent liberally. He hoisted the pack back up into the branches for safety.

An unearthly silence lay in the smothering darkness. Too many fir trees to see the stars in the sky, but full of nuts and pretzels and raisins, he slept well.

In the days that followed, his methodology seldom varied. He would paddle to a busy portage and wait. He would bring with him the unwanted remains of his last captured Duluth pack. Other campers would arrive and depart. He would smile and say hello and ruefully shrug his shoulders and claim to be waiting, telling them that his buddies were day tripping, or had gone fishing, or they were late. He would cheerfully give up his spot in line so that other campers could portage ahead of him. And in amongst the unpacking and packing, he would usually manage to switch out packs. More than once, he was even able to trade canoes. He always made sure to grab a yellow Kevlar one. He had standards.

It was ridiculously easy, and he was never apprehended.

Within a week, he had switched boats four times. He had changed the location of his base camp three times, on each occasion moving himself further north, deeper into the heart of the wilderness area.

Within two weeks, he had nearly everything he needed: a tent and a sleeping bag and an inflatable mattress, a full range of cooking gear, sharp knives, cutlery, a compass, more safety matches in little plastic Ziploc bags, more little plastic Ziploc bags, oil to cook with, biodegradable liquid for washing dishes, two more Nalgene water bottles (Justin knew he could safely drink the water from the middle of the lakes, and he could always elect to boil it, if he felt nervous).

He kept one life jacket and a waterproof poncho. He always knelt when he paddled, so the jacket was placed under his knees for support. It had rained hard several times, and the poncho had seen active service.

He had a good-quality fishing rod and lures, which snagged him a decent-sized trout early one morning, He fried it and washed it down with water stirred together with powdered orange-flavored drink, a concoction every bit as disgusting as he remembered. He had even more soap to wash himself with, a disposable razor, toilet paper, tubes of combination bug repellent and sunscreen, which he applied morning and night, instant coffee, sugar cubes, powdered milk, and lots of aspirin.

He amassed an impressive amount of returnable items: several more paperbacks (but no more Harry Potters), clothing in all shapes and sizes (but almost none his size), carefully labeled Ziploc bags filled with EpiPens and allergy medications, worthless phones with dead batteries, disposable digital cameras, lots of money and candy, a bottle of fifteen-year-old single malt whisky from the island of Islay in Scotland, and even an unlabeled Ziploc bag filled with poor-quality weed.

Justin returned most of what he found. He put the money in little Ziploc bags and placed it inside the packs. He gave back all the medications. He only kept what he thought he might need. He returned virtually all personal items. He gave back the whisky. He kept the weed.

It was on his fifth attempt to switch canoes that things almost came undone. The weather was colder than usual, and the portage was less busy than he had expected.

He waited for a sizable crowd that never materialized. He told himself he should just row away. But he didn't.

He was hailed from the shore by two teenage boys.

"Dude. You're in the wrong canoe."

Justin was in the process of making his labored getaway; only twenty feet from the start of the portage, he was still in shallow water. He turned around and paddled back.

"I'm very sorry about that," he said sheepishly. He tried to smile. "They all look alike."

And they did.

"Yours is still here, dude. It's got a different canoe number. Plus, that's my bandana."

"Oh yeah," Justin's smile was in the process of breaking down. "I guess I didn't see that."

At that, both teenagers looked at him skeptically. And why shouldn't they? It was a lime-green bandana tied to the seat of a yellow canoe. You could see it from space.

Justin was normally careful to avoid personalized stuff; packs customized with carabiners and bright-colored Nalgenes were given a wide berth.

But he had been waiting too long, and had been careless.

He had to move quickly. He continued to apologize as he transplanted the pack he had just taken. He glanced down at it in a mounting panic. But he was safe. It was a plain vanilla Duluth.

Really dudes? Canoe numbers?

Truth be told, Justin had given canoe numbers very little thought.

He had not failed to observe that every canoe on the water had a four-digit number stenciled on the side. There were several outfitting companies situated in the area, all of them with canoes to rent. Was there some way to identify from the number which store the canoe was from?

It seemed plausible.

There were plenty of canoes owned by campers themselves. They also had four-digit numbers. Justin had casually begun to look for a pattern. He didn't see it. So, he had to assume that each outfitter simply had a master list of canoes.

It stood to reason that each outfitter would know which of their canoes were hired. And which ones were missing.

Which led Justin to the question: Had his presence been noticed yet?

There was no question he'd purloined a lot of stuff. Thanks to him, packs and canoes were going missing and then magically reappearing. Some of this could be chalked up to laziness and errors. Some of it probably happened anyway. He couldn't even be sure that other people weren't living here just like him, marginalized and under the radar.

At least he hoped he was under the radar.

There were a couple of other trifling legalities for Justin to worry about.

Each canoe, rented or privately owned, had a license sealed in a waterproof double sheet of plastic and taped to the inside of the craft. The four-digit number was also written on the license. Plus, anyone canoeing the waters needed a permit, which the outfitters issued when the boat was rented.

Justin possessed a fine selection of permits. People conveniently stored them in packs. They had expiration dates, which he altered. Surprisingly, the information on the permits did not include the number of the boat.

There were theoretically rangers patrolling the waters, but Justin had encountered them only once, at the start of his trip. He had been on a stretch of popular water, near the outcrop of thirty-foot rocks that overlooked Fire Lake, where kids dared each other to jump and parents sat in their canoes and worried about injuries and liability.

The rangers were the only people on the lake permitted to use power.

Justin was approached almost before he realized they were there. He hadn't heard their engine. Which was nearly impossible given the silence. They had been lurking in a secluded bay, hidden in a drowned marsh of lilies, a matter of feet from where he had paddled past.

They signaled him to stop paddling, which he quickly did. He was asked for a permit. He handed one over. It was expired but the ranger barely looked at it. Instead he smiled at Justin.

"You're doing a fine job paddling solo," he said.

Justin smiled and thanked him.

"You camping here alone?"

Justin shook his head.

"I left my wife making our lunch."

"Where you camped?"

Justin pointed vaguely toward the further shore.

The ranger nodded approvingly. "That's a great site. Did you jump?"

Justin did his best to look embarrassed. Then he shook his head.

"Chickened out."

The ranger laughed and handed the permit back. He told Justin to have a good trip.

∞

After returning the bandana and the boat to their rightful owners, Justin paddled and portaged back to his latest remote campsite where, equipped with a knife and an eraser and a thick black Sharpie, he got to work.

The numbers were a solid black. His canoe was four-eight-eight-nine.

He thought for a while before he started.

He scraped part of the first number away with his knife, then used the Sharpie to fashion the four into a two. Justin removed half of the first eight and left the second one alone. He now had a three and an eight in the middle. The circle at the top of the number nine was badly scratched and came away easily when he applied the knife. He left the rest of the last number alone.

When he was finished, he admired his handiwork. From across the water his tampering would be difficult to notice. From a distance of three feet, it was less impressive.

But he was pleased; his customized Kevlar canoe was now number two-three-eight-one.

Justin next completed the remainder of the forgery. The license came out easily from between the two pieces of transparent plastic. He used an eraser to rub away at the letters. The paper had previously gotten wet and the numbers were already faded. He wrote the new numbers as thickly as he could with the Sharpie and slipped the license back inside the plastic.

His boat and his license now matched.

Justin moved his newly falsified canoe into its hiding spot and considered his options.

He knew he should cut down on his requisition sorties for a while. They were risky. Plus, he had stockpiled all he needed.

He had an abundance of food, a dazzling variety of packages with different pictures on the front. With few exceptions, the meals required boiling water and a lot of stirring, and tasted remarkably similar, whether advertised as Hungarian goulash or chicken with dumplings. They were, however, edible, nutritionally balanced, and would remain usable well into the next century.

He was able to catch fresh fish often. So far. He even had a fishing license. Which had expired.

He remembered fondly, from his first trip, that the outfitters sent out a selection of cheeses and summer sausage, packaged in small green refrigerated bags and meant to be consumed during the first days out.

Justin sighed. He had yet to score any of that particularly tasty booty.

Nowadays, Justin winched two food-filled packs into the air and tended to leave them suspended there day and night. He had recently decided to pull the bags up even higher than twenty feet. While he had yet to receive a bear visit (as far as he knew), he had come across more than one shredded carcass of a pack that had either not been lifted or had been lifted lower than a bear could reach. Either way, it wasn't pretty.

Two nights back, the first cold morning delivered a nasty preview of what the autumn would hold. His guaranteed all-temperature sleeping bag was easily zipped all the way up, and he was snug. By the time the sun was up, it was another warm summer day.

He drank his morning coffee cocooned inside his sleeping bag and tried to study his maps. What looked like an ever-lasting series of small portages would get him far north to Frost Lake.

The spring had been especially wet, and the water was still high. Justin knew this from paddling over the exact point where he knew a campsite should be and looking down into the depths, where he could plainly spot the metal remains of a firepit under four feet of water. He hoped that at least a few of these five- and ten-rod portages would be submerged enough to allow him to canoe over.

As he paddled north, Justin considered money, which was a matter of some irony, given where he was. In a place where you couldn't use money, he was running out of it.

As a matter of principle, Justin had elected to pay his way in the wilderness and to return any money he came across.

For example, if he found a newly purchased towel that he intended to keep, he made a guess as to its value and placed a Ziploc bag with the amount in the pack when he switched it out for the next one (he would never face a shortage of Ziploc bags).

Although he understood that his payments had little chance of finding their rightful recipients, he endeavored to be both fair and scrupulous.

Some things were too incidental; trial-size toothpastes and toothbrushes embossed with a dentist's name, a dozen Band-Aids rubber banded together, innumerable joints in—wonder of wonders—little Ziploc bags. Those he categorized as spoils of war and hung onto them.

The more substantial pieces of camping equipment he had determined were more in the nature of being a loan. When he was done, he would return the tent and the canoe and the pots and pans and the other major pieces of hardware to the outfitters.

Which raised another concern: When would he be done?

Justin had given some thought to how long he could stay in the area. This was June, the beginning of the summer. In July, the water would be warmer, and the fish would be harder to find and catch. The first two weeks of August might be the best time to be here. The water was even warmer, the air temperature was moderate, the nights were shorter, the mosquitoes died down. Edible wild mushrooms could be had.

By the end of August, the number of campers would thin dramatically.

In September, he would begin to have the place to himself. Loons in couples would make tentative plans for the flight south to the Gulf Coast. Maple, aspen, and tamarack would shift colors for the fall. It would be a place of stillness and beauty.

Justin thought he could survive until October. The ice-in would clamp down in November. By then, he would have to be long gone.

On the plus side, there would be far fewer people in the fall months. On the minus side, the pickings would diminish markedly. Would his stockpile last? There were apocryphal tales of wilderness warriors hunting and trapping their way through the cold dark months. But Justin was realistic. He had never hunted, and staying the winter would be suicidal.

He wondered if any of the outfitters staff stayed through to the spring. The gravel roads to the camp would be difficult to navigate. Was there enough cross-country skiing and snow-boarding business to keep the places busy?

He thought there might be. Perhaps a few rugged souls stayed and the outfitters remained open for business. But they would have heat and shelter and power and the internet, and he would have none of these things. He conceded that a brisk hike across ice, following the path of a frozen river with the help of experienced guides sounded like fun.

For now, his concerns remained unanswered.

COLIN

Colin left the empty urn and the canoe stranded on the raft as he threw himself into the water and swam hard back toward the house.

He was halfway there when he heard the second shot.

The sound was close and behind him. He tried to calculate where the shots were coming from. He had no idea. He dived under and kept swimming.

He made it back to the shore and looked frantically around. Should he stay in the water? He could see no one. There had been two shots. He told himself it was hunting season for something. He had no idea for what. But it was always hunting season for something.

He emerged from the water and ran for the back door. It was locked. Angie must have locked it. Good. But what could he do? He pounded. He waited. He pounded a second time. The door opened.

For a moment Colin was confused. Did it open by itself? Then he looked toward the floor. Angie was on her hands and knees backing away from the door.

She hissed at him, "Get down and crawl."

He did as he was told.

They both crouched behind the sofa on their knees. Colin was soaking the floor around him.

He asked her, "Are you alright?"

Her response was tense and short. "I'm alright."

They waited for ten slow minutes. Colin could see the clock on the kitchen wall. He was starting to chill. Angie sat with her legs pulled up to her face and her eyes tightly closed. He assumed she was furiously calculating something.

"Get up," she told him. "We're leaving."

"Can I ask?"

"Camping trip."

They stood up together and began moving slowly. They were both scared. They were both suspicious.

His question was a single word. "Hunting?"

She shook her head emphatically. "What do you think?"

He also shook his head.

"Another warning?" he suggested.

"That would be my guess."

It took them both no time to pack.

Colin was quicker, which left him time to explore. One bullet was embedded in the passenger door of his car. The second took longer to find.

When he rowed his other canoe out to the raft, he discovered that the urn was safe and unharmed. His abandoned canoe had sprung a bullet-size leak. He tied the canoes together and paddled back to the cabin.

Angie was ready to go.

As usual, Colin drove. Angie typed.

"Where am I going?" he asked.

"Duluth." There's an auto-detailing shop. There's a car rental. There's a coffee shop near both."

"Anything else?" he asked, although he knew the answer.

"There's a post office box for the Natural Boundary Foundation."

"How will that help us?"

Her response was what he expected. "It won't," she admitted. "Not remotely."

He checked his rearview mirror repeatedly, and Angie smiled for the first time in a while.

"I don't think you have to keep doing that," she told him.

"You don't think—"

"You've been looking the whole time."

"I know," he said. "I've not seen anyone yet."

Angie sighed. "I don't think you will. We got our warning. Now they're hoping we go away."

Colin drove for three minutes without checking the mirror.

Angie stopped typing.

"Have you heard of Alfred Fisher?"

Colin admitted that he hadn't.

Angie took a deep breath. "He's the best link to anything that I have so far. The NBF doesn't divulge who works for them. But they do host the occasional fundraiser. Guess where these take place?"

"Duluth."

"Who goes to the most NBF fundraisers?"

"Elliot Devine."

"Good try," Angie conceded. "He did a few over the years, not so many recently. On account of being dead. But you're wrong, anyway."

Colin waited. He used his free time to once again check the rearview mirror.

"Mr. Alfred Fisher. He's often there. Mostly looking very uncomfortable. In a cheap tuxedo that looks rented but probably isn't. In the pictures, he's usually in the center. He's usually shaking the hand of someone very rich. Fisher smiles a lot without looking happy. His teeth are horrible."

"What does he look like? Colin asked.

Angie tilted the computer screen briefly toward him.

"Is he rich?"

"He is decidedly not rich."

"What does he do?"

"He's the owner of Lauder Lake Outfitters. Guess where his business is located?"

"In the Frontier Waters?"

"Can you be more specific?"

"In the Frontier Waters on land owned by the foundation."

It was starting to rain by the time they arrived in downtown Duluth. Ted's Custom Detailing was one of three businesses sharing an empty parking lot. His shop was a two-car garage. There was a car under a huge sheet and an empty space where Colin was encouraged to park his injured vehicle.

Ted was looking at pickup trucks online. He had been expecting Colin. Angie had thoughtfully texted ahead.

His inspection of the car was cursory. "Your door will look just fine. It'll take a couple of days. I need to match the paint. You want the bullet back?"

Colin declined.

"Can I find you a loaner?"

The other two business on the lot were a U-Haul and a car rental, and they both belonged to Ted.

He checked his inventory as he spoke. "I won't charge for a beater. If you want something fancy, it will be a little extra."

Colin asked. "Will a beater get me to the Frontier Waters and back?"

Ted didn't look offended. "Sure will. All my vehicles run fine."

∞

Angie was in the coffee shop when Colin pulled up outside and entered.

"Did you want a red one?" she asked as she looked out the window.

"Ted says it's his fastest beater."

"Very impressive. Can he fix your door?"

"He seemed confident."

She changed the subject. "If you ever need to hide something, get yourself a post office box."

"You're having no success."

She shook her head, then said, "Lauder Lake Outfitters expects us tomorrow."

"What about today?"

"Too late. Tomorrow is their changeover day. It's easier to get a rental then. They're providing everything we need. I used your credit card."

"I thought we were using cash."

"That's worked so well for us so far," she sneered.

"They don't know we have a different car."

"Did you reserve it with a credit card?"

"No," he stormed back. "It's thrown in as part of the repair."

"So, we might have a mystery ride for now."

"You've been pretty free with my money."

"You're dying soon, and I didn't have much choice."

"What do you mean?" he asked.

"My credit has been temporarily frozen," she said.

"Why?" he asked her.

She answered, "I presume for the same reason my credit was checked. It's another warning. Don't worry. I still have lots of cash. And I have other accounts they don't know about."

"Which you're not going to access."

She nodded, "Which I'm not going to access. So, the rest of the trip is on your dime. Speaking of which. We have a hotel room for tonight."

∞

That night, Angela Rennie's added herself to the short list of women Colin Tugdale had slept with. Angie was only the second. Colin had been shy as a youth, to the point where his parents were resigned to his bachelorhood. Thankfully, Ruby had been certain she wanted him and was willing to do all the legwork to secure her reticent Romeo. Colin's parents breathed a collective sigh of relief; they were hoping for grand-children.

Colin's postcoital good humor evaporated at the sight of his loaner car in the hotel parking lot. It was still dark, but the lot was brightly lit, and he could see the car clearly. On the plus side, he was returning it to a man with recent experience repairing bullet holes. He noted that this one was located on the driver's side door.

On the negative side, Colin was now facing a repair charge well in excess of the car's value, retail or wholesale.

He was standing and stewing when his latest conquest arrived, carrying both of their bags and her computer.

"We're clearly not hard to find," was all she said.

"What will they do when we get to the waters?" he asked.

"Maybe they'll kill us."

"It's a good place to do it," he observed.

She looked thoughtful. "But they haven't done it yet."

"Too messy?"

"We're still being warned."

"We must be out of warnings by now," Colin said.

"Maybe we are," Angie said softly. "Maybe we are."

They said nothing else as they got in the car.

∞

They drove most of the way in silence. The big lake was at their side, lurking on the right, invisible in the predawn gloom for most of the journey north. They stopped once and bought coffee. The road was quiet as the sun finally came up, and they made good time.

At Lauder Lake they were shepherded efficiently through orientation. Their Kevlar canoe was made ready. Their two Duluth packs were filled. They had answered all the important questions: Were they decaf drinkers? Did they have any dietary requirements? Would they like bacon to fry with their eggs as part of their first morning's breakfast?

Todd worked for the outfitters. He wore an olive polo shirt. He continued to probe.

"Have you canoed the waters before?

They answered that one in the negative.

"But you've canoed before?"

They answered that one in the positive.

"How far are you planning to go?"

At this point Angie chose to deviate. "We're here to see Alfred."

Todd looked slightly amused. "Then you know he's not here." His tone indicated that these were words he had spoken many times.

"Of course." Angie looked a little offended. "We know that. We know where to find him."

Todd looked concerned. "It just seems like you might need more time to get up there and back."

Angie answered with confidence, "We can do it."

Todd pulled out a map and a pen. When he spread it out on a table Angie and Colin said nothing.

"No," he said softly to himself. "You're doing three days. In and out. You should make it. You both look pretty fit. This portage here is drowned." He pointed more than once with his pen. "And this one here. And that one there." Angie and Colin were studying his hands and the pen and the marks on the map as closely as they could. "So, you'll go there. You'll go that way. That will make it faster going." He drew a last line. "Wind is set to blow north for most of the way out. Hope it changes for you on the way back. You'll have to go through Gregory Lake at the end."

"Gregory Lake?" For a moment, Colin must have sounded less than confident. Did Todd look surprised? Angie smiled fiercely, and Todd was reassured.

"There," Todd pointed. "A long, wet portage runs out of it and there are no sites on the whole lake. But it's got to be faster going that way." Todd put his pen down. He looked satisfied with his conclusion. Then he asked, "Who did you say you guys are with?"

Angie was ready. "The Continuum Consortium."

Todd stared at Angie for a long second, his expression unreadable. "Huh," was all he said, before recovering. "Well, that's cool. I'm sure Alfred will be glad to see you."

JUSTIN

Frost Lake became Justin's best place.

He had intended to day-trip there and return to his base camp in the evening, and he did. He decided to return the next day, with one hastily packed Duluth pack and enough provisions to stay overnight.

He left early on the second day, before full light, so that he would have all day to explore the place.

There were only two campsites on the lake. One was at the southernmost point, close to the end of the last small portage. Justin had been relieved to find the day before that, as he had guessed, the majority of these mini-portages were under water and did not require either walking and/or carrying.

What had looked like six portages had been reduced to two. The larger of the two was the last one, which was still only twelve rods long. From the start of it he could see Frost Lake beckoning through a dark patch of tall hemlock trees.

With his Duluth pack on his back, his life jacket/kneeling pad strapped to the seat, and his paddle wedged firmly into the side of the boat, Justin picked up his canoe, flipped it up and onto his shoulders, and began to walk two hundred feet up and down a gentle hill, over a dense bed of needles.

It was over before it began. He was at the site of the first Frost Lake campsite.

It looked as unimpressive today as it had the previous day.

He would be moving on. Right after he had moved his bowels.

As far as wilderness man Justin Everly was concerned, camping came with one major downside. He could easily live with bugs and dirt and long portages and longer solitude. But he could kill for a clean bathroom and a toilet that flushed.

Instead of these luxuries, Justin was obliged to patronize the thunderbox, a hole in the ground with a vaguely toilet-shaped box and seat situated on top. Each active campsite had one.

The problem for Justin was that the abandoned/decommissioned sites that he favored had thunderboxes in a sorry state of evolution—or devolution. So, he chose to do his crapping on the run, using active campsites like rest stops, picking when he could use the more popular ones and then swiftly moving on.

But there were some instances where he could not be so choosy. On the edge of Frost Lake, at the conclusion of an absurdly easy portage, nature called.

The path away from the campsite toward the thunderbox went uphill and was demarcated by the rotted remains of an old paddle propped against a tree and crowned with a roll of toilet paper sealed tight and dry in a Ziploc bag. This was expected camping procedure. What was unexpected was the thoughtful addition of a red disposable lighter and a rolled joint secreted inside the bag.

What also bucked tradition was the presence of a small rucksack lying against another nearby tree. Justin took the plastic bag and its contents up the path to the makeshift toilet.

He also took the rucksack.

As custom dictated, he laid the paddle on the ground

across the path to indicate both occupation and the desire for privacy.

At the end of the path, he sat down with his swim shorts around his ankles and fired up the joint. The view was unexpectedly far and the weed was both fresh and of exceptional quality.

From where he sat, he could see beyond the hemlocks an example of the controlled burns that took place each spring. A section of nearby woodland was mostly charred stumps standing like gravestones, garnished with only the sparsest of new forest greenery.

He had exhausted the views from his throne. There was no longer any refuge from his curiosity.

He opened the rucksack.

Inside was yet another large Ziploc bag to add to his stash. Inside the large Ziploc bag was a handgun.

Had Ruger GP100 not been clearly visible on the side, Justin would have been unable to identify what he held in his hand. It looked brand new. Justin knew enough to recognize that the gun was a revolver. It was surprisingly small and heavy. Justin's hand wasn't especially big. The wooden handle fitted cozily inside it.

Justin opened the cylinder and found exactly what he expected to find. He removed the bullets without daring to breathe and then carefully closed it. Once it was closed he looked for a safety catch on the gun. There didn't appear to be one. He put the bullets inside the bag.

Then he made himself breathe again.

Justin felt a little sick. Whether it was finding a loaded gun, or the fact that he hadn't smoked decent weed in a while, he was unable to say.

He and his friend Dylan had shot sporting clays with the church kids once. He'd had fun, and he'd shot well for a first-timer, he was told. It had been a cold spring day. They had drunk hot chocolate with little marshmallows in paper cups afterwards. He'd never gone back.

In the days following the trip, several church parents had questioned the appropriateness of a church-sanctioned shooting activity. Not the parents of the kids who had attended the shoot; those parents had all signed permission slips. Justin had, as usual, forged his father's signature.

Justin finished the joint and walked back toward the campsite and the lake. He lifted the paddle from the ground and replaced it against the tree.

He was still holding the gun and the lighter and the toilet paper and two Ziploc bags.

He put the gun inside the bag with the bullets, and the toilet paper and the lighter in the other bag, before placing that bag back on the top of the paddle for the next patron. He opened his Duluth pack, placed the Ziploc with the gun and the bullets inside, and closed it up.

Had he forgotten something? He looked around, then waited until it came to him: He'd left the rucksack at the thunderbox.

He considered his options. He'd taken everything that was inside it. He could leave it where it was. He could put it back where he'd found it. Or he could take it with him. He made up his mind quickly.

∞

Justin considered himself an expert in assessing the amount of use portages and campsites received. The short portage to Frost Lake was rarely frequented, as was the first campsite. Given the beauty of the lake, Justin was surprised, but, as he considered the remoteness and the paucity of campsites, he was less surprised.

And yet this remote spot boasted a handy bag with weed and toilet paper provided. Plus, a shiny new weapon.

At that moment Justin arrived back at the facilities. The rucksack was right where he left it. He picked it up and looked inside. As he had thought, there was nothing else inside. The bag looked new. He thought for a split second of leaving some money inside it for the gun, and he almost laughed out loud.

That weed had been strong.

He decided to take the rucksack.

Justin noticed that the path to the thunderbox went a little way past it, and this he followed for as far as it went, perhaps another fifty feet or so, when it abruptly came to an end.

Another thing that Justin was rapidly becoming expert at was sensing, mostly with the aid of his nose, the presence of recent death. He sensed it at the end of the path, and when he considered whether to explore more, to determine the natural (or otherwise) source, or to take off, he chose the latter.

With the empty rucksack safely secreted in his pack, newly armed and unexpectedly stoned, Justin Everly set sail across Frost Lake, away from the smell of death and his own shit.

∞

The second campsite was situated near the midpoint of the lake, on the western shore. There was a spit of sand running perpendicular to the coastline, with a wooden table and two rows of bench seats constructed in one solid piece and anchored into the outstretched sand. Further inland, beyond the sand spit, stood a raised rock outcrop, with a fire pit plainly visible near the summit.

There were three trees on the rock; all pines in raggedy condition.

Justin had been to the site yesterday. There was a stronger breeze on the water today. There would be an even stiffer breeze up there. And there would be few insects. He had brought a tent, but he weighed sleeping out on the rock tonight. It would grow cold fast, but he had his toasty sleeping bag to zip up in.

It was the prettiest place on the prettiest lake, and he had it all to himself.

COLIN

Colin and Angie left the outfitters with their Duluth packs on their shoulders. Todd had arranged for their canoe to be put in at Selkirk Lake. He thought that Selkirk would give them more time to get as far as Alfred. They had signed up for a three-day/three-night trip. It was Monday morning; they would come out early Thursday morning.

They walked side by side in silence down the narrow path toward the dirt parking lot where the outfitters van awaited them. Beyond the lot, the path grew wider, and the descent was steep all the way down to the edge of the water. It was just past six in the morning.

There was one canoe strapped upside down onto the trailer behind the van. Wordlessly, they walked toward it. There was no one in the van yet.

Angie spoke quietly, "See any bullet holes?"

Colin shook his head. He didn't.

"There could be a bomb hidden inside."

He considered ignoring her. "It would be hard to hide."

"Once we get out there, we will be exposed."

He said nothing.

"They could kill us."

"They could have killed us already."

"Yes," she admitted, "but it'll be easier out there."

They both watched as a teenage girl in shorts and an outfitters shirt walked toward them, holding her coffee and smiling. She looked nothing like a killer.

The outfitters would be a zoo by mid-morning, but Colin and Angie had been the first customers. The place would remain civilized for a few more hours.

An old golden dog was fast asleep under a strange tree. The animal had found itself good early morning cover. Although the leaves were already exhausted from the summer heat, they were still large and flat and mostly green. Underneath the leaves, gnarly branches twisted and curled in on themselves. The tree was no more than ten feet tall and about the same width.

Neither of them knew what kind of tree it was.

If the dog knew, he or she wasn't saying.

∞

As they climbed into the canoe for the first time, they could see no visible bombs attached to the inside of the boat.

Todd had been right. The wind would be at their backs as they canoed the length of Selkirk Lake.

Soon, the steady stroke of their paddles grew soothingly hypnotic. Close to the shore, Colin watched the reflection of the waves shimmer against the smooth side of a tree. In twenty minutes, his neck was sore. Colin was in back. Angie was in front. He had asked her to choose a side. She chose the left and proceeded to row exclusively on that side. He rowed on the other to keep their course straight; when he needed to steer the canoe, he switched sides with his paddle. She had been told to switch over when she grew tired, but he wasn't convinced that she would admit to fatigue.

They had already met up with a posse of tourist-friendly ducks. They offered the birds nothing in the way of treats, and the scavengers swam huffily away. Colin spied an otter on the shore before it scampered under a log. They heard the shriek of a faraway loon.

They pulled out into the middle of the lake and the silence of the wilderness became louder, more physical, more invasive.

Colin thought he could still dimly hear the growl of the outfitter vehicle, as Tawni (for that was their would-be murderer's given name) drove the truck through rolling clouds of dust and dirt back to Lauder Lake.

Simultaneously, he and Angie stopped paddling for a second or two. At that moment, ten feet or so from the canoe, something had broken the surface and splashed once, before sinking back down. Colin guessed a large fish. The lakes were reputedly well stocked. Todd had claimed that lake trout and walleye were easily caught and made for excellent eating. But they were in a hurry, and neither of them could fish, so they had declined the option of ultralight fishing rods. They had regrets. They both liked walleye.

After a while, Colin couldn't conjure up the comforting illusion of noise, beyond the rhythmic slice and splash of the paddles.

An hour later, they had voluntarily tangled themselves up in something less an island and more a natural anchor; an outcrop of mossed rock with a slender branch reaching toward the sky. It seemed an appropriate place for them to stop and drink some of their water and to talk over what it was they had both wanted to say since they had set sail.

"My hand will be one huge blister soon."

"It's amazing out here."

"We have a long way to go before dark."

"Did you see where Todd pointed to on the map?"

"I did."

"I did, too."

"It's a long way."

"It is. Can we make it?"

"I think so."

"I think so, too."

Then there was a brief mutual round of stammering along the lines of, "Last night was . . . it was . . . I just . . . thank you," before the awkwardness ended.

"Todd was much more helpful than he realized," Colin said. "That was all thanks to you. How did you—"

Angie smiled at him. "After I found pictures of Alfred Fisher at the NBF fundraisers looking uncomfortable, I kept looking. I found all these other pictures. There were a lot more Lauder Lake Outfitters pictures. I noticed that in many of them, he was meeting people out in the waters. He looks a lot happier out there, with his camping and fishing and all that Ernest Hemingway stuff. I gambled on that. And we won. We got here. And Fisher's out there some place where we can find him."

"But you made it seem like we knew where he was."

"Maybe. Maybe not. I'm not sure Todd was paying that much attention, so our bluff got past him."

Colin thought of something else. "Did you notice that the route up through Gregory Lake looked like a longer distance?"

"Yeah," she said. "It didn't just look like a longer distance. It is a longer distance. But I added up the portage distances, including a monster one at the very end to get to the place where Fisher likes to hang out. Todd's route has more water."

"It should be faster."

She nodded, "Yup."

"The Continuum Collective?"

"Consortium."

He snorted at that, "Whatever."

Angie explained. "Their name just came up more often. He meets with them the most. I also noticed that the people from Continuum kept changing. There were different faces each time. Sometimes there were women at the meetings. I thought that was unusual, because Alfred Fisher mostly likes to go camping with white men who represent companies with goofy new age names. Which seems nuts. He owns an outfitter. He should be meeting with folks who make waterproof tents and dig toilets and stuff like that. Instead he hangs with people who represent secret organizations with bullshit names. They all use words like *continuum* and *synergy* and *paradigm*. Even the term *natural boundary*. What the hell is that meant to be? And they all have these websites with fancy pictures of pretty places and not much else. I think they're all a collection of hippie naturalist weirdos. But, I don't know, maybe they're worse."

"How worse?"

"Maybe I'm the one who's paranoid, but the more I think about the words *natural boundary* the more I imagine white men with pointy white sheets over their heads. Did you see the look Todd gave me when I told him who we were with?"

Colin concurred, "I did."

"And?" she pressed.

"I have no idea what that meant."

"Me neither. But I was sure I'd screwed up. At first, he looked surprised, even alarmed. Then he looked like he liked it."

"You're reading an awful lot into one look."

"Maybe," she allowed. "Or maybe not."

"Suppose he's not out there?"

"We keep looking."

"We don't know what we're going to find."

"We never did."

"So why are we doing this?"

She burst out laughing, "You're just asking that now?"

"I am." He waited stubbornly. "Well?" Still nothing. "Why?"

Angie took a deep breath. "Okay. Elliot Devine should be dead. I should be sick or dead. Someone out there doesn't like attention. The NBF is too odd. We're both stubborn. We both like mysteries. We're doing something that saves us all the awkward conversation people have when they first start dating. And then—"

"And then?"

"Nothing."

"You can say it."

"Okay, I'll say it. We're helping you."

"And how is that?" he persisted.

"We're helping you get over losing the love of your life." She rinsed out her Nalgene bottle in the lake. "Would you come back here for a trip? Just for fun? Without all this stuff?"

"With you?"

"Well, obviously with me."

"In a heartbeat."

"We should do it soon."

"Don't say it."

"Because you don't have long."

Colin deftly flicked his paddle across the surface of the lake and a spout of water hit Angie squarely in the face.

∞

The first portage out of Selkirk Lake was easy to find. It was a two-hundred-rod distance that would connect Selkirk to Big Lake. They were aware they would encounter longer and shorter portages. Before they began the first portage, they stood in silence to consider the logistics of their trip.

They were two fit people, with two packs, two paddles, two life jackets, and one canoe. Their life jackets were tied to the canoe seats for added rear padding, and their paddles were firmly wedged down the sides of the boat.

Angie positioned the canoe on her shoulders as Colin strapped one pack to his chest and the other onto his back.

Angie's challenge was balance and maneuverability and the threat of low-hanging branches.

Colin's was one hundred pounds of evenly distributed weight, added to the fact that he could no longer see his feet in front of him.

Colin stumbled and fell once. Failing to see a tree root. His front pack hit the ground first and spared his face from contact. From there it proved difficult to get his hands past the pack on his chest and push himself up. So, he flipped over onto the pack on his back. And in that ridiculous position, came to know exactly how a turtle felt, flipped onto its shell with all its meaty parts vulnerable and exposed.

He quickly rolled back onto his chest pack and waited for the cavalry to arrive.

Angie was right behind him. She pinned the front of the canoe into the ground and twisted her way out from under it. Then she grabbed him by his pack and unceremoniously yanked him to his feet.

"The person carrying the canoe goes first from now on," she announced. "They can look down and spot any rocks and roots on the ground." Angie flipped her canoe up and back onto her shoulders with ease. "Do you want to take the canoe for the next portage?"

"I don't want to think about the next portage."

They finished the portage without Colin falling again. At the end, they were hot and tired, so they drank more water and splashed around in Big Lake until they had cooled down enough to continue.

"Where are we going next?"

"We canoe the length of Big Lake," said Angie.

"Then?"

"Lunch."

"Good. Then what?" he asked her.

"Short portage."

He was instantly suspicious. "How short?"

"Eighty-two rods."

"You call that short?" he snorted. "Then what?"

"Roscommon Lake."

"How long is that?"

"Longer than Big Lake."

It didn't make sense that the lake next to Big Lake would be bigger than Big Lake.

Angie was in the back of the canoe doing the steering and navigating this time.

At the far end of Big Lake, the water merged into a lily pad. According to the map, the portage to Roscommon Lake lay just beyond the lilies.

Any semblance of a breeze died as they paddled into the tangle of round flat plants. They followed the clear demarcation where other intrepid campers had plowed into the heart of the plants and carved out a six-foot-wide lane that would lead to the start of the portage.

Without a word of discussion, they began to paddle. Instantly they felt warmer. Streams of bubbles burst from the depths. Flies became more plentiful, but Colin and Angie were well insulated in a thick marinade of repellent/sunscreen.

The lily flowers exploded in dark pink petals. The plants themselves were rooted in the shallow soil plainly visible under the water. Occasionally, their paddles bumped against the bottom.

The width of the channel kept changing. Neither Angie or Colin wanted to damage the leaves, so they drifted through the narrow passages and then paddled harder when the water grew wider again.

At one point, they heard birds crying overhead.

"They sound like seagulls," Angie said.

"Herring gulls are common here. They like the marsh-lands."

"And you know this because—"

"You do remember that I live not far from here part of the year."

She changed the subject.

"I should be more scared than I am."

"So, why are you not scared?"

"It's just too amazing a place. We have to come back later in the year. I could stay up here forever."

Then she changed the subject again.

"I think our map is wrong." Angie had carefully folded the paper so that the section they were canoeing in was visible through the transparent plastic wrap. She was staring at it. Colin had stopped paddling and was sipping his water. He stopped.

"Why is it wrong?"

"Because the water is too high," she explained. "Look ahead of us. That's not a portage. It should be a portage. It looks more like marshland. Which would explain the presence of seabirds."

"So, afterward, our portage should be shorter." He sounded pleased.

She agreed, "It should. But the marsh will be slow to paddle. We might have to partially portage some of it, which will be muddy and messy. It might not be any faster going than the full portage would have been."

Angie's prediction proved accurate. They plowed the canoe into the slurping mud several times. The flies mounted a fresh assault, as the effectiveness of their repellent wore thin. At several points they clambered onto the bank and dragged the canoe and their packs across alternating clumps of rotted wood, slimy subsurface rocks, and a soup made of equal parts dirt and grass.

They fell over. They fell down. They fell in.

"Still want to stay here forever?" he called out.

Angie wiped thick mud from her eyes. She said nothing.

Their portage to Roscommon, when it came, was much shorter.

∞

Angie took the two packs. It was Colin's turn to balance the canoe on his shoulders.

They had intended to eat before leaving Big Lake, but the ill-defined area where the marsh morphed into portage was unappealing. There was a grimy thunderbox situated at the end of a twisty path. There was no available paper, but they broke out their own double-ply stash from the top of one of the packs.

Next, they embarked on their first wet portage, one extended puddle of muddy water interrupted by sodden heaps of fallen trees. At points during the miserable trek, they could feel the presence of long wooden slats under their feet, now grown treacherous and slippery.

For one blissful stretch, they were elevated onto a wood-plank bridge that the water hadn't reached. That section of the portage was dry and relatively easy to navigate, although Angie's progress was hindered by the caution she was required to demonstrate; it was a long drop if she stumbled and missed a plank.

Colin walked with the canoe in front. His eyes fixed on the bridge. If the path changed direction, he would let her know.

The portage ended abruptly at Roscommon Lake. There was a breeze blowing across a section of sand and beach, and, suddenly, they had a choice location for their late lunch.

They were in a hurry. Their bacon and eggs could wait for the next morning and breakfast.

Angie broke out pita bread halves and stuffed the still-cold sausage and cheddar cheese inside. Colin paddled further out and brought back two Nalgenes replenished with drinkable water. Inside the cold packs, they discovered four chocolate chip cookies for dessert.

After a short post-lunch swim there was the length of Roscommon Lake to traverse.

JUSTIN

He woke the next morning to the sound of loon screams breaking the silence at first light. The breeze had lasted the length of the night and he had slept well under a gallery of stars he was unable to identify.

As he waited for the water to boil, he watched a beaver cross Frost Lake. It made good progress as it cut open the glass surface; an expanding V spreading out behind it. Justin pulled out his map. The beaver was making for a point midway up the eastern side of the lake, where an inlet marked the end of a long portage from a small lake without a single extant campsite, past or present.

He had been studying his map before he fell asleep.

It was surprising, at least to Justin, that Frost Lake could only boast two campsites. In his mind he had already given them names. This one was Sandspit Camp and the one at the end of the short portage into the southern end of the lake was Gun Camp, for obvious reasons (although he had considered Good Weed Camp, Big Dump Camp and Dead Something Camp).

He hadn't liked Gun Camp. It was too close to the portage and to the edge of the water, there were too many trees, and the ground was marshy.

When his coffee was ready, he returned to his map. Frost Lake had none of the customized markings that Justin used.

Except for his visit yesterday, he knew nothing about it. He wanted to know more, and he had the whole day ahead of him.

∞

By lunchtime his map had acquired new lines.

To begin with, there was a passable trail between Sandspit and Gun which, without the handicap of a pack or a boat, had taken him an hour to complete. It had been hard going in places, a large Douglas fir was down, which required scrambling over, but it was not as rough as he thought it might be. He passed an isolated area of severe storm damage, and noticed subtle signs that the trail showed use, which was curious given its remoteness. As was his habit, he tried to measure out the distance in rods as he walked. It came close to one thousand, which he calculated to be around three miles.

He turned right back around as soon as he reached Gun. It wasn't any more scenic than it had been yesterday, and he was thinking about the smell at the end of the trail and about the contents of the rucksack.

For the rest of the morning, he had paddled slowly along the western edge of the lake north of Sandspit. His canoe was almost motionless for long stretches, as he studied the coastline for anything unusual.

As picturesque a campsite as Sandspit was, Justin had no intention of making a basecamp out of it. For one thing, it was exposed. For another, it was identified on the map. In addition, he'd noted that, as remote as Frost Lake was, Sandspit was surprisingly well used.

Justin wasn't a born tracker, but he was attentive and he was thoughtful. Some of the camps gave every indication of having had stampedes of careless campers descend upon them, with each cleared area having housed a tent, with careless attempts at holes with discarded food clearly visible, with young green wood left cut down and unburnable at firepits, and even the occasional beer can or candy wrapper lazily discarded. These were evidence of both population regularity and density.

But Sandspit was different. The campsite was used prudently. There was the well-flattened grass that indicated the regular placement of a single tent. A small pile of logs stacked thoughtfully beside the pit. No wrappers. Nothing left behind. Almost no trace.

Justin suspected that Sandspit was used by just one camper, which seemed unlikely and strange.

Suddenly, Justin stopped paddling altogether. He drifted to a stop.

Although he couldn't define exactly what was different, he instinctively knew that the place he was looking at had once been a campsite.

Justin's collection of maps now went back over several years, and this location, close to the northernmost point on this lake, on one of the northernmost lakes in this section of the wilderness, had never been designated as a campsite on any of them.

So how was he so sure?

In his mind he scrolled through a checklist of favorable criteria: the exposed rock, the elevation, the palpable scarcity of vegetation, and the relative ease of approach. It boiled down to the simple consideration: Would I want to camp here?

Justin found that, when he could answer his own question with a rousing affirmative, he would discover that his opinion was the seconding of previous travelers' views.

He took one last stroke before letting the canoe drift into a wedge between two rocks that seemed custom made for it. As he walked up the hill, he felt a breeze stroke his face. He saw a handful of trees that he mentally catalogued, gauging the distances for hanging his tarps. He made a rough estimate of how visible he would be from the water. When he lifted the canoe out of the water, was there a secluded spot for dry dockage? Could you see it from the water? Were any of the tree branches suitable for raising his packs above bear level? He had already both tasted and approved the quality of the lake water. He looked back toward Sandspit and Gun. There had been a number of small bays and inlets cutting up the shoreline. Neither Sandspit or Gun were visible from the top of the hill; ergo, his new campsite would not be visible from either of them.

This was all to the good.

He stood at the highest point and looked down at the ground, noting the remains of a firepit.

He made up his mind in an instant. This would be his new campsite.

Justin's next days were guaranteed to be wretched because he needed to move all his stuff.

The question was how. Ease of transport or fewer trips? He could load his canoe to the point where there was barely room for him. The paddling would be grueling, and he would have to portage in stages, leaving his packs abandoned and exposed. But he was tempted by the thought that the whole process would take only a day—one long and labored day. On the other hand, he could move one pack at a time. He could canoe with ease and traverse each portage in one trip. This method, he estimated, would take three days.

Either way, there was a bright side. He had reached the furthest edge of the wilderness, as planned, and he would have a wonderful new campsite. The trip north to Frost Lake was less portage-infested than many he had made, and his worst hike was under one hundred rods.

In addition, there was a spring-cleaning opportunity. He would evaluate everything he had amassed. Would he need another towel between now and November? Why did he have more than one set of nail clippers? Since he finally possessed the first Harry Potter book, should he read it?

He decided he would use all three days to make his move. This would take longer but would be physically less demanding. He would be more visible in transit, but his supplies would be better hidden at each end.

His mind was made up.

COLIN

Colin and Angie arrived later than they would have liked, but they had left Lauder early, taken advantage of putting in at Selkirk, paddled hard, and skimped on portage time. As a result, they were the first canoe of the day to make it as far as Roscommon, and they had their choice of several attractive campsites for the evening.

"We take the one with the highest elevation," Angie told Colin. "More breeze. Fewer insects. Better view of the lake. Better view of other people on the lake. More time to take evasive action after spotting said people."

There were three good prospects at the far end of the lake. They had time to canoe close to all three. Angie quickly made her choice. Colin was mystified.

"They all look nice," he told her.

"One has garbage," she pointed out.

"We could pick it up. Or we could burn it. Or we could bury it."

"I know we could. It just . . ."

He pressed her, "So, the other two . . ."

"One of them is higher."

They looked the same elevation to Colin.

"It is!" she said much louder.

He wasn't convinced.

"It just looks—Okay, I just like it better."

They were both tired, and, even though it wasn't yet the end of the day, they made camp for the night.

Their canoe was pulled out of the water. Bacon and eggs for dinner had won by unanimous vote. Colin was declared dinner chef.

They erected the tent, started a wood fire, strung a rope and hung a tarp between two trees, washed their swimsuits and left them spread out on the side of the rock to dry in the late sun. Their sandals were beside the fire and were already dry. They had blown up their mattresses to the anemic-looking maximum recommended pressure.

Colin had chosen the site for the tent. He had unpacked everything he needed for their dinner. He had yanked their Duluth packs a full twenty feet into the air and then tied them off.

He was now busy cooking dinner. Angie was naked and discreetly submerged, furiously scrubbing at the layer of sunscreen and insect repellent on her body.

They had metal plates and plastic cups. Their eating utensils all clipped together. They had paper towels that they would pack away and bring back with them. Anything they didn't eat, they would dig a hole for and bury. They (or more accurately, Angie) would painstakingly wash their dishes a recommended safe distance from the lake to avoid water contamination.

As much as possible, they would leave no trace.

Colin looked ruefully at the plastic cups.

While Angie had been using the restroom back at the outfitters, he had quickly made a purchase, which he had hidden inside one of the packs.

She returned, scrubbed raw, in her pajama shorts and a fresh T-shirt. Her feet were bare. Colin had also dressed for dinner.

He chose this moment to reveal his surprise.

"You brought wine," she squealed.

He smiled modestly, "They sold some at the outfitters."

It was a relief to find that the cooking supplies included a corkscrew.

The plastic cups would have to do. He poured the wine.

They toasted the lake and each other and bacon and eggs. Then they toasted Ruby Tugdale.

They planned to sit late into the night and sip their wine and watch the stars and listen for the wailing of evening loons and good-naturedly lie to themselves and to each other about what they would do after they had finished their journey.

They got as far as their first cupful, agreeing that tomorrow they would take a day trip. They would pack enough food for two meals in one of the refrigerated bags with the last of the meat and cheese. It would go much faster without the two full packs to manhandle.

They both loved this campsite. They would come back late tomorrow night and sleep and then get up the next day and head back. It occurred to them that they might not have enough time to do it all. They hoped to find Alfred Fisher. But what would happen if and when they did find him? They didn't know. They did know that, in a million different ways, things might go badly. At the very least, it was possible that they may not make it back to Lauder Lake as scheduled. Was there a penalty if you arrived late? Surely, they would not be the first campers to misjudge the time needed to journey back.

It was important to find Alfred Fisher. They already knew exactly which lake he liked to frequent, so it was a gamble with acceptable odds.

This was as far as they got with planning and talking and lying.

They were both too exhausted. Tomorrow, they would start early.

CONCLUSION

Their next day blurred into walking and rowing and sun and water and mud and flies.

By the midpoint in the afternoon, Colin and Angie had finished a final, long desolate portage out of Gregory Lake. They stood on the eastern side of the last lake of the day. This was what they intended would be the northernmost point of their trip.

There were only two campsites on the lake. One was directly across from them; a pretty location on the side of a rock bluff. Angie had better eyesight, and she could make out a wooden structure on the edge of the water. It had the appearance of driftwood piled up high. She thought an intended beach fire, although the construction appeared too deliberate and permanent.

There was no sign of campers. The wind had stiffened and was blowing from the north. The lake was wide.

The map indicated another campsite close to the portage into the lake from the southern end. It wasn't visible from where they stood. It was a shorter canoe, and the prevailing wind would be in their favor.

Colin spoke for both of them.

"Fisher might not even use a campsite."

"I agree," Angie said. "But we should check them."

"Do we try the southern one first?"

She considered, "It's the easier canoe. And once we get there, the wind might change for us."

"Which one would you stay at?"

She smiled, "That's easy. The one straight across. I think I can even see a beach."

"That's a hard paddle across."

"I know. And we're tired. If we go south first, the paddle up the western side might be easier. We can keep to the shore and be out of the wind. Come on. Let's get going."

Did it seem as if their decision had been made too quickly?

They both considered that possibility as they paddled south. A few minutes later they could see the southern campsite. It didn't look promising.

The canoe was much lighter and easier to maneuver with just the two of them. As the wind pushed at their backs, Colin and Angie found they barely had to paddle. Colin told himself that the next time they came here, he would take a tarp and some rope and their two paddles. He could fashion a makeshift sail, and they would use the wind to propel them. He could do it. He had sailed before. He understood the general concept.

It was a fine day, and Angie was laughing. Her voice carried far across the water.

It was no great surprise that the southern campsite turned out to be an ugly place; low and flat and marshy, under a dark suffocation of trees. The lake breezes deadened. There was a thunderbox situated at the end of a path. There was toilet paper, but the walk to the facilities smelled strongly of death and decay. Colin would have preferred to wait, but his twisting innards argued.

Angie was left to explore the site, which she determined was not occupied. She thought it might have been recently.

She already disliked the place, and she resolved to leave this lake the way they had entered it, through the portage on the eastern side, strong and unforgiving wind or otherwise.

She bent down to touch the scattering of ashes in the firepit. As she stood up she stretched her arms as high as she could.

The high-powered hunting rifle was a deadly weapon that required only one clean shot. And when it came, Angie Rennie's heart exploded.

She was dead before she hit the ground.

∞

Colin heard the shot as he stood up. He ran back as fast as he could. He reached her and he fell to his knees. He lifted her up by the shoulders and held her tightly. When he looked at her face, she was still smiling. There was dirt on her cheek. Blood was soaking out through her shirt as Colin began to sob.

He was still holding her when he heard the voice. It was very close.

"I'm afraid your friend ran out of warnings, Mr. Tugdale." The voice betrayed no emotion.

Colin looked up at the sound to see a man carrying a rifle balanced in both hands, making his way slowly through the trees. As the man got closer, Colin recognized Alfred Fisher.

Fisher spoke again, "You should sit down and make yourself more comfortable Mr. Tugdale."

Colin looked wildly around. He could run away. He could run to the canoe. He could run into the woods. And he would be shot in the back whichever way he chose. Or he could attack Fisher. The man was holding the weapon loosely. But then Colin thought he saw Fisher's hands tighten.

Colin would be too slow. Whatever he did. He would die in the woods. He would die in the woods with Angie. He looked down at her. She was still bundled in his arms. He was soaked in her blood. He tried to think.

Colin looked up at the man as he sat down. Alfred Fisher wore thick olive trousers and an outfitter T-shirt that hung loosely on his thin frame. His hair was trimmed short and was mostly gray. He wore heavy boots. While he looked to be about Colin's age, there was something about him that seemed much older. They were both fifty-five and they were both not fifty-five. But Alfred Fisher was more not fifty-five than Colin.

"You will be happy to know that she felt nothing, Colin."

Breaking his silence, Colin asked, "How do you know me?"

"The foundation has been watching you both for a while." Fisher seemed happy to be in a conversation.

"Why did you kill her?" There was no emotion in Colin's voice.

"She was stubborn and much too resourceful to be allowed to live."

"Will you kill me?"

Fisher seemed surprised at the question, but said, "Almost certainly."

"So, why don't you?"

When Fisher smiled, Colin saw his soiled and uneven teeth.

"That can wait a while. I thought that Ms. Rennie was the more dangerous one. But you might also pose a danger."

Colin fell into silence again.

When Fisher spoke again his tone was expansive.

"I must say I'm a little surprised that you don't want to know who I am?"

Colin answered dismissively, "I know who you are. You're Alfred Fisher. You own the outfitters. And you're a member of the foundation."

Fisher pretended an air of vagueness. "Very good. All mostly true. I run the foundation. But forgive me. I should've been clearer. Don't you want to know who I was?"

"I don't understand you."

"I used to be quite famous, Mr. Tugdale. They called me the Weld Wizard. I'm Sir Julian Brand."

"Brand died," Colin said harshly.

He laughed, "Oh, I can assure you, I did not."

"Then you welded," Colin said.

"I did a little better than that," Alfred Fisher/Julian Brand smiled. Then he continued, "I suggest you lay your friend on the ground, Mr. Tugdale. She's not going anywhere. Sit for a while, and we can talk. Then you can try to escape, and I can kill you. It's funny. I was sure that she was the real danger. But now that I consider it, I don't think Ms. Rennie would have ever gone to the authorities. She was a very clever criminal. But a criminal all the same. She needed to stay hidden. You, on the other hand, Mr. Tugdale, have so much less to lose. Your time is almost up. Your lovely wife has already concluded. You have lived most of your All Clear Twenty. A good life, wouldn't you say? A clever and wealthy son. But maybe I'm still wrong. Do you want to live a little longer?"

Colin said nothing.

Brand looked at him. "Colin? May I call you Colin? You do want to live. I can see that now. You're watching me carefully. You see that I have the rifle. You could attack me, if you were quick. And you look quick. You might have a chance. But I don't think you want to risk it. You have no wife, no partner, and less than two years left. But you still don't want to die. Remarkable. I almost want to let you live. And I could let you live. I could even let you live longer. A lot longer. But no, you are going to die. It might be quick, and it might be cruel. It might be a little more sporting. But first, you must have lots of questions, and I feel like talking."

Colin calculated. It would do no harm to talk. It would buy him time to think and plan, and it would be instructional. He took a good look at Brand's rifle. It looked modern. It had a telescopic sight attached. It looked deadly.

"What happened to you?" Colin asked.

Brand barked out a laugh. "Ah," he said. "The big question. Are we stalling for time? And why not?" He pretended to ponder. "Where to begin?"

Colin waited and watched.

"We created the scan and the weld, as you know. And then we, or rather I, decided to give the technology away. To every king and queen and prince and president. We offered it free. No questions asked."

"And they took it?" Colin asked.

Brand snorted, "They did, indeed. Naturally they took it. Why on earth wouldn't they? There was just one tiny proviso."

"Which was?"

"I was to be left alone. Guaranteed. In writing. A binding contract. To last for as long as I lived. And that was the genius part of the whole caper."

"They all signed."

He nodded. "Every last tyrant and tin-pot dictator. They each got free access to the weld. The Geneweld Mark One, that is."

"Mark One?"

"I have a question for you. Other than tinkering with computer games with your son, how much actual science do you know, Mr. Tugdale?"

"Almost none."

"Then let me give you the potted version. The first version of the weld lasts twenty years. The All Clear Twenty. You are about one year short at this point. You would agree that it has worked as planned. Your scan was clean. You were offered a settlement. You were lucky to live where you live. Your government paid you well. Your health has been perfect. If you do nothing, you will die. And that is exactly what is supposed to happen with Mark One."

Brand paused and shook his head.

Then he continued, "All the governments wanted to come up with their own timeframes when I first offered the weld. But I told them that the twenty years was not negotiable. There would be a two-decade window of healthy life and then death. I told them that this was how the weld worked. I said I had no control over this. I told them I was sorry if that was inconvenient. They grumbled, but not for long. How could they turn down my offer? Perfect health for two decades? When they stopped grumbling, they asked my opinion on the matter of when to weld. I told them that fifty-five seemed like a good idea to me. They went along with that."

"Which part was a lie?" Colin wanted to know.

"Not so much a lie. The truth was that the weld I provided them with does last twenty years."

"And you got to play God with them."

"Of course I did, Mr. Tugdale. Who wouldn't want to play God if they could?"

Colin said nothing.

"And then I got to keep right on playing God."

"You welded yourself," Colin said.

"Naturally."

"How many years did you give yourself?"

"I gave myself the Geneweld Mark Two. I have all the time in the world."

"Who else has Mark Two?" Colin asked.

Brand seemed surprised at the question. "At first, no one else. Just me."

"Weren't you worried that you would get old and lonely?"

"Oh no," Brand grinned. "I think not. I don't suppose you've heard of the Brand? I thought of the name myself," Brand said. "Clever of me. Don't you think?"

He received no comment. He continued.

"You will like this part, I think. You and your son, Tony. You helped him create a fiendishly clever computer game. Very popular, too, as I understand."

Again, Colin said nothing.

"I created a second version of the weld. Mark Two. This is what I called the Brand."

"What does it do?"

"Oh, nothing much, Colin. It works very much like the weld. With one critical difference. The Brand lasts forever. There is no All Clear Twenty. There is only perfect health forever for those lucky enough to be Branded."

Colin asked a question to which he already knew the answer: "You've Branded others?"

Brand grew expansive. "There are people, Mr. Tugdale, that I have come to know. We find ourselves in accord on many of the important issues. They have come to be my friends. They share my views. They have come to me, and I have Branded them. They will now live with me forever."

"How do you know you can trust them?"

"That's easy. I mentioned you and your son. My fiendishly clever computer game is an implant that resides in their bodies. I planted it there. When I Branded them. If they disappoint me, they will die with a simple computer command."

Colin could think of nothing to say.

Brand burst out laughing, "Does it not sound wonderful? And all very James Bond in the bargain. Don't you think?" He continued to laugh.

"And you Branded them? Just like you Branded yourself?"

Brand stopped laughing. He smiled.

"And why on earth would I not?"

"How many?"

"There are currently twenty-four of my Brands out there. No, there are twenty-three. I always forget about Devine. Did you notice a nasty smell near the privy?"

Colin slowly nodded.

"And you and Ms. Rennie were anxious to locate Mr. Elliot Devine."

Colin nodded again.

"I'm afraid he's the source of the smell. He is in the process of returning to nature. Of giving back. Of personally recycling."

"You killed him."

"I prefer to think I revoked his opportunity to live forever."

"You shot him?"

"You know, I really did consider using the plant inside him. But no. You're right. Shooting him was more fun."

"What did he do wrong?"

"He wasn't able to give the foundation all his money. As he had promised. His greedy crew of women saw to that. He failed miserably at living in hiding. As you can attest. But the error was also mine. Devine loved aspects of nature, but he wasn't a true naturalist. There is a difference. I wanted financial security for the foundation. I took a stupid chance. I'm afraid that Mr. Devine wasn't our type."

"What is your type?"

"I'm surprised you have to ask. You and Ms. Rennie visited our website when you weren't trying to sneak your way into our financial records. We believe in a natural boundary."

"What does that mean? Your website says nothing."

"That is as intended. Our website is for the casual observer. Our membership exists much deeper in the web. We believe that nature is the only thing that endures. We believe that our form of naturalism is the preordained order of things. The preordained order of things is for men like me and my chosen friends to rule the world. Which we will do, someday. We are superior, and our superiority is now plainly manifest in our ability to live forever. We will pick our moment to rule. There is no hurry."

"Are all the Brands white men?"

"They are," he smiled.

"You disappeared a long time ago."

"That part was easy. I always loved camping. So, one day I went camping. And the next day, I vanished. Simple as that. Presumed dead. Of course, I wasn't dead. I came up here. I started the outfitter business. It's done quite well. Pays for itself. I love it here. We have the tourists all summer, but the winter months belong to me. Marvelous country. Wouldn't go anywhere else. I live a pretty private life. I can hide up here for long spells. I've changed my appearance a little. Nothing too drastic. There is one thing that makes me hard to recognize."

"The teeth?"

"Yes! Very good. Lucky old Sir Julian had the finest set of gnashers, and now I have to endure these monstrosities. But somehow, they manage to hide me in plain sight. Who would've thought?"

"What happened to Angie's Parkinson's?"

"Excellent question. There are a number of unexplained outcomes of the weld. One unfortunate aspect is its ability to cure Parkinson's in black people."

"Why is that unfortunate? Why doesn't the world know about this? It would stop suffering."

"Sir, you assume I care what happens to black people. I don't. Ms. Rennie was a thief. A clever thief. She stole her weld. It gave her a few good years without her disease. She was a very lucky thief. She was warned to stay away from the foundation. She chose not to. Now she's dead, and I say good riddance."

"You do realize you're racist and sexist and insane?"

Brand stopped smiling.

"And you will die in a year or so. Or sooner. If I feel like it. Do you have more questions?"

"I do."

"Then you should have been a little more polite. We're finished talking now." He raised the rifle to his shoulder. "So. Here is my question. Are you ready to die?" He didn't wait for an answer. "I hope you are. This was question number one. Would you like to die right now? Number two. Would you like to run for a while and then die? Number three. Would you like me to be a good sport and count to ten? That was question number four."

"These are my only choices?"

"Yes."

"Will you count to ten for me?"

"Of course, I will. Would you like me to count quickly or slowly?"

"Very slowly, please."

"As you wish. And thank you for saying please. I shall bid you goodbye now, Mr. Tugdale.

"ONE."

Colin laid Angie gently down and got to his feet. He looked around.

"TWO."

He thought he remembered the direction from which Brand had come.

"THREE."

Colin turned quickly. He was now facing that direction. Brand nodded and smiled in approval, as he made a small adjustment to the sight on his rifle.

"FOUR."

Colin took off into the darkness of the trees. Was this a path? As he ran as fast as he could, the ground dipped, and he almost fell face first into a small tree. He windmilled his arms to stay on his feet.

"FIVE."

Colin kept running. How long should he keep on the path? He intended to hide somewhere. Where could he hide?

"SIX."

This was the last number Colin heard. He thought he was still on the path. He glanced down at the right moment. He had just enough time to jump over a fallen branch. He cleared it by a matter of inches.

Seconds later there was a rifle shot.

Colin heard it clearly.

Brand had finished counting.

By his own frenzied reckoning, Colin was heading north on what he still thought of as a legitimate path. He was jogging now; the slower speed allowed him to listen for Brand behind him. He could hear nothing.

Shortly, he was surrounded by isolated devastation: uprooted trees plucked from the earth by a localized storm and then casually scattered. There were deep holes where the roots had been torn up. Colin chose the dead tree furthest from his path and threw himself into the damp cold darkness underneath it.

There he lay for several minutes, while he tried to breathe more slowly and think faster.

Angie was dead. She had been shot and killed by an insane man with the power to keep other insane people like him alive forever.

Colin was still alive. For now.

There was another site on this lake. Further north. It had looked to be the prettier of the two. Perhaps Brand was making his camp there. It made sense. He knew this place. It was his kingdom. It stood to reason that he would stay at the other site. He wouldn't want to make his camp where Angie lay dead, where the body of Elliot Devine was decomposing.

Colin was on foot. He thought it was possible that Brand was, too. But that wasn't necessarily true. Colin's canoe was back at the site where Brand had shot Angie. It was possible that Brand would use it, that he was out on Frost Lake. Had there been another canoe there? Colin couldn't remember, but he didn't think so. If Brand was in the canoe, it would explain why Colin couldn't hear anyone behind him.

But if he wasn't on the water . . .

Colin thought he could more easily make his escape on water. He knew the route back to the outfitters. And his car was still there. He could drive away. All he had to do was get back to Lauder Lake first. The fastest way back had to be by canoe.

But Brand owned the outfitters at Lauder Lake.

He had lived and camped here for years.

He was healthy and psychotic.

He had a powerful weapon.

And he wanted to kill Colin.

As Colin hid inside his root hole, he considered his limited options. The possibility that his death was close at hand was inescapable.

Colin wondered if Brand might already be heading south back to the outfitters where, once he got there, he could sit and wait.

Colin had few illusions about his chances on foot in the wilderness. He preferred his odds on the water. If he continued on foot, he would too easily become lost. And if he didn't become lost, he would still be exposed in a microworld governed by a man with a gun who wanted to kill him.

Even if the man who wanted to kill him was crazy, he was right about one thing.

Colin Tugdale wanted to live. He wanted to bury Angie someplace better. Not at that campsite. Not where she lay.

He could double back. Perhaps that would be the last thing Brand would expect. He could take her body with him, and he could take their canoe. If it was still there.

Somehow, he could do all this and still get away.

Colin remembered the smile before he started to run, and he thought he understood it. Brand had seen him look toward the direction from which he'd come. He would expect him to keep running in that direction. Colin thought that the path might lead to the other campsite on the lake. That seemed possible. But what would he find there?

He could keep on running north.

But he could also double back. For the canoe. And for Angie.

He chose the latter.

If it had been possible to walk on his tiptoes, Colin would have done it. As a result, he made agonizingly slow progress. But his sense of direction was good, and he was able to retrace his steps all the way back to the campsite.

He looked for a sign of pursuit. He listened carefully for the evidence of another person nearby. But there was none.

Now that he wasn't running, Colin was engulfed in clouds of insects. His route went steadily downhill, into a dense twilight of dark, the air exponentially wetter and much closer, as any errant breeze from the lake was suffocated.

He soon arrived back where Angie lay. Their canoe was still abandoned, plowed into the mud at the side of the water, only feet from the portage they had elected not to take. Would it have made any difference if they had come this way? Would Angie still be alive if their journey had followed an alternate route?

She lay where she had fallen.

He sat on the ground beside her.

He touched her face.

Her skin was beginning to cool.

He reached out and closed her eyes.

Colin heard a twig break behind his back.

Brand emerged from behind a tree with his rifle raised. When he spoke, he sounded sad. "I've learned to never underestimate the power of rank sentimentality. Let me guess what you did. You hid for a while. Then you pretended to consider the available options. But it came down to the fact that you couldn't bring yourself to leave her here."

He shook his head before he continued, "I never considered giving chase. I fired my gun like a starting pistol. But I needn't have. You had already taken off like a frightened rabbit. I liked your spirit at first. You saw where I came from and you chose that path. You assumed that it would lead somewhere. And it does. Had you kept running, you would have found your way to the other site on this lake, by the way. One of the more picturesque spots. I have often camped there. And I still will." He sighed dramatically. "I had hoped for a lengthy hunt to the death, Mr. Colin Tugdale. But you disappoint me. Now you will die as Ms. Rennie died."

Colin was finally able to speak.

"Why are you doing this?" he asked. "Why are you keeping people like yourself alive forever?"

"Because, as I told you, one day my good friends and I will decide to rule the world."

"And when will that happen?"

"Heaven only knows," he laughed. "That's the wonderful thing. Don't you see? I have no idea. But it doesn't matter. We can afford to wait. We have all the time in the world. I shall say goodbye, now. Consider this your conclusion. Isn't it appropriate that it's delivered to you by the man who made conclusions possible? Only one year ahead of schedule."

Colin got to his feet. He could only watch mutely as the rifle was raised.

But the sound of the gunshot, when it came, came from further away. The first bullet hit Brand in the arm. He looked around, his expression a mixture of indulgence and mild confusion. When the second shot hit nothing at all, he smirked. The third bullet entered his brain though his temple, leaving him permanently oblivious to the fact that the last two shots also missed their mark.

His lifeless body hit the ground no more than ten feet from where Angie Rennie lay.

At that moment, Justin Everly, holding a pistol loosely in his hand, began to walk slowly toward Colin and the two bodies on the ground.

The two men faced each other. It would be hard to say which one looked more tired.

Justin was the first to speak. "I recognized him. He was the English guy. When I first camped here. He owns the outfitters up here. He looks the same. His teeth are still bad. He seemed okay then."

Colin answered, "He's not okay."

Justin nodded. "That's good. Because I just killed him." He pointed to Angie. "He killed her, didn't he?"

Colin nodded.

"Why did he do that?"

"Because she was very clever."

"Was she your friend?"

Colin nodded again.

"Then I'm sorry for your loss."

"Thank you for killing him. Why did you do it?"

"I could hear some of what he was saying. He seemed bad. He was going to shoot you. So, I shot him. I heard the shots a while ago. It took me a while to get here. I'm glad I made it."

Inexplicably, at least to Colin, Justin Everly held out his hand.

"When he said your name, I was sure you were the good guy and he wasn't."

"I beg your pardon?"

Justin Everly looked bashful. "When he said your name. I recognized it. Your son is Tony Tugdale. Trench Warfare is the best shooter game ever made."

Despite the events of the last few hours, Colin smiled and shook his young savior's outstretched hand, offering a silent prayer of thanks to the gods of e-sports.

Some hours of daylight remained.

It didn't take Justin long to find the liquified remains of a body near the campsite thunderbox. It didn't take Colin long to arrive at the conclusion that this was the final resting place for Elliot Devine, an entrepreneur, and a nature buff who cheated death once, then refused to play dead.

After a cursory examination, with their noses held, both Colin and Justin stood convinced that his body was not going to be identifiable anytime soon.

They dragged Brand's body to the same spot and threw it on top. His rifle was still in his hand. They left it there. Justin wiped his own prints from the pistol and placed it in the dead man's other hand.

Colin hoped the acidic stew that constituted Devine would speed up the decomposing process of Brand's corpse. He knew the weapons used to kill both men were locked in death grips, and that the identities of both men would prove interesting to the authorities, if they happened upon them while anything was left to identify.

Beyond the path to the thunderbox was an area of controlled burn that Colin had not noticed before. Charred tree stumps stood like gravestones surrounded by ash and desolation. It occurred to Colin that there was almost nothing left living in this place.

He would take Angie away from here.

Before they abandoned the site, Colin and Justin carried her body to the canoe. Justin thought they should bury her at the other site further up the western shore of the lake, at the top of the rock, overlooking the beach and the wooden table. Justin said it was pretty.

They dug long into the night, too scared to stop for fear of not being able to dig deep enough before it got dark. Colin labored at the job for hours; his anger powered his effort, the physical toil distracting him from the urge to lament and the temptation to place the blame for Angie's death on himself.

Before they started digging Justin had washed her blood from inside the canoe before paddling to his own abandoned site further north on Frost Lake. He had returned with two shovels. Before he left, he found Brand's canoe with two Duluth packs still inside. He apparently hadn't made camp yet, abandoning his stuff after spotting Colin and Angie across the water as they entered the lake from the side portage.

Like the old pro he was, Justin went through the two packs when he returned with the shovels. What he found was utilitarian, the only luxury item being a laptop computer that lacked both a power source and an internet connection but which was, nonetheless, an interesting find.

Justin packed it away.

Colin continued to dig.

Justin had brought flashlights and batteries.

When Colin was done, he gently placed Angie's body inside the hole and covered her.

Justin chose to speak only when Colin had finished tamping the ground flat.

"Do you want to say something?"

Colin shook his head. "No," he said. "Not now. I'm coming back here tomorrow. To make it look nice. I just wanted her to be safe for the night."

Colin's last sentence emerged from somewhere inside a sob.

Then both were silent.

Justin navigated the canoe back to his campsite in darkness. Before they left, they loaded Brand's two Duluth bags back into his canoe and tied it behind their craft. They decided they would move his possessions to Justin's site that night, and transport them to the southern site tomorrow, where they would dump out his belongings as unceremoniously as they had dumped his body.

They agreed they would keep the laptop until they got back to the outfitters, and make that trip south together, after Colin had tended to Angie's grave and said his goodbyes.

The next morning, Colin was relieved to discover that Angie's grave had survived the night undisturbed.

He found a large smooth rock to use as a headstone, which he covered in wildflowers. He carved her initials into it as best he could, and he spread a thin layer of wood scraps and leaves and more flowers over the soil, so that the ground wouldn't look so freshly excavated.

When he finished, he was happy with the result.

Before he and Justin left, he looked out across Frost Lake.

Justin had been right. When the morning sun landed on the water, it was very pretty. Most of the lake was visible. Tiny waves patted the wood frame of the picnic table on the beach, and it was possible to see the finger of sand that stretched under the shallow water and out into the deeper reaches.

Colin felt certain that Angie would have loved it.

From the start of the journey, the two men made good time. They left Brand's canoe overturned in the marsh water at the southernmost campsite, his Duluth packs stripped of all perishables, which were then tossed on top of the two bodies to encourage reluctant wildlife to dine.

They were left with one canoe and Colin and Angie's cooler pack to transport.

"I'll come down with you," Justin said as they started to paddle. "But I'm coming straight back up."

"If I'm returning the canoe," Colin answered him. "How will you get back up?"

Justin smiled.

They reached Colin and Angie's previous campsite and packed up the remaining gear.

Colin and Justin made a formidable team. Justin had become a sinewy master boatsman, and Colin was still fueled by twin propellers of sadness and rage.

They paused only for the shortest of meals, and they paddled and portaged long hours into darkness.

At one point, they stopped paddling to drink water. Colin watched a hawk in the lake water close to shore, washing its tail feathers obsessively. The process took forever. What did it need to wash away? Fresh blood from a recent kill?

When it was done, it flew to a tall tree and sat high in the branches shaking its feathers for as long again.

Finally, it flew away.

Both Colin and Justin thought it would be a while until the authorities began to look for Brand. They both thought that what they would find would keep them occupied and perplexed.

But they were taking no chances.

They knew the sooner they got to Lauder Lake, the better.

On their second night together, right before they fell asleep, they talked.

"What will you do, Justin?" Colin asked.

"I'm staying here."

"In the winter?"

Justin hesitated. "I don't know about that yet. Probably not."

"You could move into town."

"I'm thinking about it. I like Duluth. And I thought about going back to college."

"Where did you live before?"

"It doesn't matter. I'm not going back there."

There was a long pause.

"Do you have any money?'

Justin anticipated what Colin was thinking. "Why would you want to do that?"

"I have some. A lot. You could have some of it. I'm going to die soon."

"But why?"

The answer seemed obvious to Colin. "Because you saved me."

Colin managed one final thought before he fell asleep. "If you need more money after that. After I go. You need to get in contact with my son. With Tony. He'll expect you. I'll tell him about you. There will be a bank account set up. It will be there for you."

Justin thought of a question to ask Colin, but he was too late.

Colin was sound asleep.

When they got back to Lauder Lake, the outfitter was too quiet for Justin. There were no crowds in which to hide. The exposure made him uneasy.

It was the end of the week. There were a few tourists looking to camp, but mostly the area was populated by outfitter employees in their telltale olive shirts, fixing up abused canoes, washing out empty Duluth bags, refolding tents, and scrubbing out pots and pans.

Colin was late back with his canoe and thus obliged to pay for an extra day. The smile on the young woman's face as she ran his credit card told him that it happened a lot.

"Welcome back to civilization," she said as he signed papers and retrieved his valuables from a safe.

"Where's your partner?" she asked.

Colin thought fast. "Waiting at the car," he said. "She's dirty and she thinks she smells and doesn't want anyone to see her." He tried to laugh convincingly.

The young woman smiled, "Tell her she can shower here."

Colin shrugged, "She just wants to get going. You know how it is."

She finished up the paperwork, and Colin was free to go.

Justin was waiting outside the office. He was sunk into an Adirondack chair as he held Brand's computer tightly in his lap.

Both men were suddenly very hungry.

Colin bought sandwiches and sodas and a long power cable for the computer. As he handed over his money, Colin wondered how much the staff at Lauder Lake knew about their employer. It wasn't something he could ask.

When Colin found Justin, the younger man stood up reluctantly. He stretched his body upward then groaned loudly.

"The one thing I miss the most? Up here in the wilderness?"

"What's that?"

"Back support."

Colin smiled sympathetically.

They found two other chairs further away from the offices, affording more privacy and shade. There was a charging station nearby, equipped with multiple outlets.

"My rental came with two complimentary showers," said Colin. "That's something I missed."

Justin considered this information. "When we finish this. If it works out. We can both shower. I must be dirty. Way more than you."

"Do you think it will work?" Colin was holding the laptop.

"You're good with computers," Justin reminded him.

While that was true, Colin wanted to say he was nowhere near as good as Angela Rennie had been.

How long would her death take to rise to the surface? She was a criminal and secretive, and she was cunning. He thought it might take a while. She had relatives. He would try to find them when he got back. He would stop first in Duluth to exchange cars.

They ate their turkey sandwiches and drank sugary, ice-cold sodas.

When they finished eating, they powered up the laptop. Colin held it. Justin watched over his shoulder as he began to type.

The welcome screen asked him for a four-digit password.

Colin Tugdale almost felt like laughing. He punched in the numbers without thinking. Nothing happened.

He tried again. Still nothing.

Colin began to panic. How many attempts could he make before he was locked out? He forced himself to slow down and think.

"Type one-two-three-four," Justin said pleasantly. "Most people are lazy. Or arrogant."

Colin wanted to argue. But he entered the numbers.

Just like that, he was in.

Justin asked, "What numbers were you using?"

Colin mumbled something about a stupid hunch and began to type.

Most of what they found on Brand's laptop was related to the Natural Boundary Foundation. Spreadsheets documented financial scenarios both lavish and spartan. Brand had been fantasizing about Elliot Devine's bequest before his chances of landing it vanished.

Colin studied all the applications on the laptop. He thought he knew most of them: browsers and notetaking programs. He read through lists of contacts. There were several hundred, mostly people unfamiliar to Colin. He found one name he recognized. There were copies of credit reports concerning one Angela Rennie. They were extensive; well beyond lists of tardy payments. Other documents related to her. He found one email where Brand had requested that her house be broken into and searched. He even found his own name, noting that his status was never elevated beyond harmless sidekick.

On a secondary screen, Colin found an unknown application with a one-word name that initially meant nothing. He paused and considered the word. It seemed like it should be something significant. So, he thought harder.

Then it came to him. It was the name of the university where Sir Julian Brand and his team had discovered the scan/weld.

He clicked on the icon and waited.

It was too good to be true, an exact number of names. All twenty-three.

All men. The ones Colin recognized were as white as driven snow.

Several were known violent racists. Others were survivalists. A select handful swung both ways.

One was a high-ranking politician with an unimpeachable record.

Two were third world dictators infamous for the brutality of their respective regimes.

And as far as Colin could remember, they were all dead.

There were a few names that meant nothing to either

Colin or Justin. Colin would have been more than happy to ascribe guilt through association, to generously wager that the names that failed to register were not the names of justly sainted philanthropists or Eagle Scouts.

Instead, he used his phone to check for obituaries, which didn't take long, as internet service was blindingly fast close to the outfitters.

He read quickly. As he suspected they had all been eulogized, mostly castigated, and only occasionally mourned.

Beside names in the spreadsheet were dates. Colin's best guess was that he was looking at activation dates for the Brand. The dates of their "deaths" varied. Similarly, the dates of their unholy rebirths were randomly assorted.

Unbelievably, up above the names was a menu bar with a number of irresistible options. He clicked once on Edit. From the drop-down menu he chose Terminate. Then he held his breath. The names reappeared with a select box beside each name. He clicked them one by one. Then he clicked Continue. After he had done that, he was asked again if he wished to continue with the termination process. The options were two large buttons marked yes and no. A warning at the bottom of the screen strongly implied that once the yes button had been selected there was no going back.

And there he stopped.

Colin could hardly speak. He whispered, "I think this will terminate them."

"Are they all killers?" Justin asked quietly.

"I don't know. Maybe. I'm not sure."

"Do they all deserve to die?"

"How should I know?" Colin said. "I'm not God."

Justin marshalled his thoughts. He tried again.

"There were names that you recognized," he pointed out.

Colin nodded slowly.

"Were they all evil? The ones you knew?"

Colin nodded again.

Justin asked, "Can you tell how old they were when they first died?"

Colin used his phone once again.

"The names I recognized on this list are all men who lived to be at least seventy-five."

"What about the other obituaries?"

Colin could see where this was going. "They all concluded," he replied.

Justin chose his next words carefully. "Then they all should be dead by now," he said.

Colin looked at the list again, at the names he knew. He struggled to recall his first encounter with each name, watching footage of right-wing agitprop rallies that morphed into pitched battles, or seeing shadowy websites exposed by liberal media watchdogs. He grew surer. They were all gruesome men.

Colin raised a last argument. "We shouldn't get to play God."

But Justin swept it aside. "Do you want to let them live?"

"No," Colin said. "I don't."

Justin spoke. "Then don't," he said.

Colin looked down at the screen. He had taken too long. He reselected them all. He was asked to choose yes or no. Once again, he chose yes. He was asked if he was sure, if he was certain he wanted to terminate the chosen names. He indicated that this time he was.

With one last implausible click, it was done.

Colin Tugdale was a god.

∞

They had the communal showers to themselves.

There was no shortage of hot water, which was good, because they were both filthy. Especially Justin, who was vigorously bathing himself again. He scrubbed away at the strata of dirt/sunscreen/repellent that was lacquered onto his bare feet.

When Justin Everly had looked into a large mirror, he was surprised at his appearance. His body was lithe and sinewy, and his face was weathered. He thought he looked simultaneously ten years older and twenty times fitter.

From behind the shower curtain he talked loudly to Colin, who had washed and shaved and now sat on a wooden bench bundled up tightly in two rough towels.

Colin had been doing some thinking.

"Tony and I could help you buy this place."

"Is it for sale?" Justin was starting to laugh.

"It might be," Colin said. "I understand the owner just died."

"That's interesting," was all Justin said.

"You know how to contact me?" Colin asked, not for the first time.

"I do," Justin replied.

"Let me know where you are after the summer. Email me."

"Like I said. I thought maybe Duluth."

"What would you do there?"

"I know how to tend bar. Deliver newspapers. Work in a diner."

"You mentioned college before."

"I did," Justin said. "I meant it."

"What would you study?"

Justin had his answer all ready. "Nature. Ecology. Biology. I like living things and living places."

When Justin turned the water off, there was a warm, steamy silence.

"There is one thing," Justin began.

"What one thing?"

"Something you could do for me."

Colin waited.

"Are there any cheats?"

"Cheats?"

"In Trench Warfare?"

Colin hesitated. He had promised Tony. But he spoke up, anyway.

"Have you fought the First Battle of the Marne yet?"

Justin informed him that he had.

"And did you march through a French town afterward?"

"I think so."

"Did the citizens throw flowers?"

"Yeah. I remember now. They did."

"There was an old lady dressed in black. She was standing in the street. She was handing out yellow flowers to the soldiers."

"I don't remember that," Justin said. "What about her?"

"You need to fight the battle again. When you win and your troops march through town, the old lady will run out into the street and hand out her flowers like before."

"What do I do then?" Justin breathed.

"You shoot her in the head."

"Well, I can do that," Justin said with a grin. "But what happens then?"

Colin Tugdale was unable to stop himself from smiling. "You'll see," he replied.

ACKNOWLEDGMENTS

Shirley Murray suggested rearranging the chapters of this book. She improved it immeasurably in the process.

Rick Hanzelin arrived at the very last moment, and made the northern wilderness that much more believable.

All the errors that remain belong solely to me.

PETER ROBERTSON was born and raised in Edinburgh, Scotland, and currently lives near Chicago.

GIBSON HOUSE PRESS connects literary fiction with curious and discerning readers. We publish novels by musicians and other artists who love music.

GibsonHousePress.com
❑ GibsonHousePress
🐦 @GibsonPress
◎ @GHPress

For downloads of reading group guides for Gibson House books, visit **GibsonHousePress.com/Reading-Group-Guides**